THE WHITE ROBIN

Also by Miss Read

VILLAGE SCHOOL

VILLAGE DIARY

STORM IN THE VILLAGE

THRUSH GREEN

FRESH FROM THE COUNTRY

WINTER IN THRUSH GREEN

MISS CLARE REMEMBERS

COUNTRY BUNCH

CHRONICLES OF FAIRACRE

OVER THE GATE

MARKET SQUARE

THE HOWARDS OF CAXLEY

VILLAGE CHRISTMAS

FAIRACRE FESTIVAL

MISS READ'S COUNTRY COOKING

NEWS FROM THRUSH GREEN

TIGGY

EMILY DAVIS

TYLER'S ROW

THE CHRISTMAS MOUSE

FARTHER AFIELD

BATTLES AT THRUSH GREEN

NO HOLLY FOR MISS QUINN

VILLAGE AFFAIRS

RETURN TO THRUSH GREEN

MISS READ

THE
WHITE
ROBIN

Illustrated by
J. S. Goodall

LONDON
MICHAEL JOSEPH

First published in Great Britain by Michael Joseph Ltd
52 Bedford Square, London WC1
1979

ISBN 0 7181 1775 1

Set and printed in Great Britain
by Ebenezer Baylis and Son Limited,
The Trinity Press, Worcester, and London
and bound by Redwood Burn, Trowbridge and Esher

To Macdonald Hastings
who gave me the idea

Contents

1 The Visitation   9

2 The Odd Man Out   20

3 Snowboy   36

4 Bitter Weather   48

5 A Nest of Robins   60

6 Our New Pupil   71

7 A Tragedy   78

8 Fairacre Mourns   90

9 A Second Shock   102

10 The Long Wait Over   116

CHAPTER 1

The Visitation

Village schools get rarer every year, but there are a small number, up and down the country, which still look much the same as they did some hundred years ago.

Fairacre School, where I am the headmistress, is one of them. It has, in common with many other country schools, the inestimable joy of a playground where the surrounding countryside invades the small patch of asphalt.

How lucky we are! The town child goes out to play at break-time on a vast, arid waste, criss-crossed with painted lines for various games, and rarely boasting even one desiccated plane tree. He would be hard put to it to find even a modest wood louse in this desert, whilst we in Fairacre enjoy the company of the birds and insects which share the trees, the meadows and the cornfields around us.

We are blessed with a fine clump of lofty trees which gives us shade at one side of the playground, a hedge of hawthorn and hazel which provides cover for the birds, and a dark corner where the playground touches the adjoining garden wall of the vicarage.

This secret haunt is the favourite place to play. Here grow, in wild confusion, all those rank plants and shrubs which flourish on neglect.

Elder trees, their bark criss-crossed and green, wave their ghostly flower heads in the shade, and fill the air with spicy scent.

On the vicar's side of the flint wall, mounds of rotting grass cuttings have accumulated over the years, providing a perfect habitat for outsize stinging nettles and majestic dock plants which raise their rusty spires above the wall. Little ferns grow from the crevices and, along the top, strips of moss like velvet ribbon flourish between the ancient coping bricks. Here and there great swags of ivy hang down on each side, the twisted ropey stems providing footholds for the inquisitive ones wanting to peer over the wall.

On our side of the wall, the same plants thrive, but we also have some blue periwinkles and some particularly hardy yellow aconites which some long-dead gardener must have introduced, and which seem to enjoy their murky surroundings.

Above all, spreading its arms in general blessing upon ecclesiastical and scholastic territory, is a superb oak tree, drawing nourishment, no doubt, from the vicar's grass cuttings and from the neighbouring churchyard with its mossy headstones.

Invariably, there are a few children enjoying this

shady retreat. It is a fine place to rest after a spirited assault on the coke pile at the other side of the playground. There are always plenty of snails there, some small and elegant with pale yellow and brown shells, and many more of the common or garden variety, laboriously clambering up the wall and leaving their silver trails across the flints.

And in their wake come the birds. Blackbirds and thrushes, wrens and robins, raucous starlings and ubiquitous sparrows all haunt the bushes for food, and also for places to nest in this delectable spot. It is no wonder that the children find it so attractive. Around them stretch open cornfields and meadows. The great bulk of the downs lies on their horizon some two or three miles distant. Under a vast sky, the open countryside shimmers in a heat haze in summer and endures the onslaught of bitter winds in winter. This enclosed and secret place, mysteriously quiet, the haven of shy wild things, is in complete contrast to the bracing downland in which they live, and is prized accordingly.

And it was here that one of the Coggs twins first saw what I brusquely dismissed as 'her vision'.

It was a day of July heat, with the end of the school year in sight. The schoolroom door was propped open with a piece of sarsen stone as big as a child's head. We had already used the object as the theme for a useful lesson on the derivation of words, although I had the feeling that my explanation of 'Saracen', meaning a foreigner, turning into 'sarsen' had been only partially accepted. In this heat the children were more than usually lethargic, their minds running, no doubt, on the joys of the open air rather than the schoolroom.

From outside came the sounds of high summer. A posse of young blackbirds kept up a piping for food, following their hard-working parents, tattered now with weeks of child care, hither and thither across the playground. In the distance the metallic croak of a pheasant could be heard, and over all was the faint hum of a myriad flying insects.

The languorous hush was broken by Helen Coggs who raised a hand. It was the usual request, and I was swift to grant it. The Coggs children seem to need to visit the lavatory twice as frequently as the others, but they are poorly fed and poorly clothed, the product of two feckless and unhealthy parents, so that their little weakness is not surprising.

'You can take out your library books,' I told the class, as Helen vanished across the playground. It was pointless to try and compete with the heat. My efforts to enliven the derivation of 'sarsen' had met with so little response that I felt that their library books might offer more palatable food on a hot July afternoon.

While they turned the pages languidly, I busied myself with some marking at my desk. I had forgotten about Helen, and it must have been some ten minutes later when she appeared at my side looking unusually lively.

'Oi bin and sin a whoite bird,' she declared. The fact

that she had seen a white bird did not excite me greatly. It was probably a seagull, I thought. They come inland when conditions are rough by the coast. Or maybe one of Mr Roberts's white Leghorn hens, or a goose, had strayed.

'You've been long enough,' I scolded, 'Go and get on with your reading.'

Somewhat dashed, the child returned to her desk and took out her book. Peace reigned again, and I continued to mark.

But some minutes later I put down my red pencil. There was something odd about this white bird. Gulls would not be inland in this weather and, now I came to think of it, Mr Roberts, our local farmer, had given up keeping chickens over a month ago. He still had a few geese, I believed. Could one have strayed so far?

'This bird,' I said to Helen. The class looked up. 'How big was it?'

'It were a little 'un.'

'It wasn't one of Mr Roberts's geese?'

'No.'

'You're sure it was white?'

'Yes.'

'Well, come on! Tell me how big it was.'

The child put her hands three inches apart, but said nothing.

Like getting blood out of a stone, I thought despairingly. Most of the Fairacre children are barely articulate. The Coggs children are monosyllabic at best.

The rest of the class now began to take an interest in the proceedings.

'Could it have been a white blackbird?' I enquired. Some years earlier we had been visited by a partially albino blackbird. At this my class began to guffaw.

'A *white* blackbird!' repeated Patrick, pink with mirth. 'How can a *black* bird be a *white* bird?'

'You sometimes get a blackbird with a few white feathers,' I explained, but the children were far too busy enjoying the joke to take much interest.

The clock told us it was playtime, and I decided to shelve the problem. In any case, no fowl of Mr Roberts seemed to be involved, which was my first concern. Also I had a suspicion that the white bird might have been some other object, a piece of paper fluttered by the wind, or a white flower head. With some of the children I might have suspected that the bird was a figment of a lively imagination, but not with Helen Coggs. She was quite incapable of such a flight of fancy.

The children streamed out into the sunshine, their spirits brightened by the prospect of fresh air and exercise, and the enjoyment of Helen Coggs's disclosure.

'Some ol' magpie, I bet,' said Ernest derisively, as he passed her on his way out. She shook her head.

The classroom soon emptied, except for Helen.

'Run along,' I said.

'It were a *little* bird. On the vicar's wall. Up the back.'

This was one of the longest speeches I had ever known

the child deliver. 'Up the back' was the term used affectionately to describe the bosky haunt I have described. The lavatories are nearby, and the child must have spent some time after visiting them in exploring this much favoured area. But a white bird? Much more likely to be a head of elder flowers, now in full bloom, caught by an eddy of air and visible briefly over the wall. I must get the school doctor to test the child's eyes on her next visit.

'Don't worry about it,' I said. 'Go and enjoy the sunshine. If there is a white bird about, you will probably see it again some time.'

What a hope, I thought privately, as Helen moved off. It was highly unlikely that the apparition would be seen again.

But it was.

This time the vicar saw the white bird, and hastened into the school to report the sighting. The Reverend Gerald Partridge visits our school regularly, not only because he is chairman of the managers, but because he is our parish priest and the friend of all Fairacre.

Having told me the news in some excitement, he turned to the class.

'I've just been telling Miss Read that there is a rare white bird about. No doubt some of you have seen it?'

The children looked at each other in silence. Then Ernest nudged Helen's shoulder.

'I sin 'un,' muttered the child.

'Where, my dear?'

'Up the back.'

The vicar turned to me for clarification.

'By your wall,' I explained. 'Where the elder trees grow.'

'Ah! And all the weeds! Yes, I suspected as much. The robins must have nested there again this spring.'

'Do they nest there every year?'

'I can't say with any certainty, but the vicarage garden always seems to have one or two pairs each year, and very little fighting over territory. I imagine there is enough room for all. One pair built in the ivy on the wall some years ago. We found the nest later.'

'And are they there again?'

'Somewhere there, I feel sure. There are so many ideal sites in that wilderness, and we have certainly seen three or four fledglings being fed recently.'

He turned again to the class.

'Now, this little white bird seems rather shy, and it may well be attacked by other birds as it looks so different. I want you to be very careful not to frighten it in any way, and to let Miss Read, or me, know if you catch sight of it again.'

'Is it a foreign bird then?' hazarded Patrick.

'No, my boy. I rather think it is a robin – an *albino* robin. Albino means that it has no colour.'

Here he paused.

'At least, albino birds are usually all white, but in the case of the robin or the bullfinch the *red* feathers still keep their colour, so you can see how very beautiful a white robin must look.'

There was a stir of excitement among the children. A white robin, with a red breast! Here indeed was something rich and strange!

'I intend to find out more from Mr Mawne,' he told my class. Henry Mawne is an ornithologist of some standing, and lives in Fairacre. He is a good friend of the vicar's, and the church accounts have benefited from his meticulous attention. Before his coming they were in sad disarray, as our lovable vicar has no head for figures, and since the advent of decimalisation has been more bewildered than ever. Henry Mawne has relieved him of his financial duties, and the village is grateful to him.

'Perhaps he will come and give you a talk about birds – particularly robins. I will ask him. I know he has some splendid slides of British birds.'

He said goodbye to the children, and I accompanied him into the lobby.

'And you think this really is an albino robin?' I asked.

'I'm almost sure. I've caught a glimpse of it twice now, and the second time I had my binoculars. Its breast is quite a pale golden colour at the moment as the bird is so young, but it was being fed by a true robin, I'm positive. Isn't it exciting?'

His face was radiant.

'Think how beautiful it will look by next Christmas! We must take great care of it. I'm sure you will impress upon the children how fortunate we are to have such a wonderful bird among us.'

I promised, and was about to return to my class when the vicar stopped me.

'But you knew already, I suppose, about this bird? I mean the child Coggs said she had seen it.'

'I'm afraid I didn't believe her,' I confessed.

'Didn't believe her?' echoed the vicar, looking shocked. 'But she is a truthful child, surely?'

'She's truthful enough,' I agreed. 'But it seemed such an odd thing to see,' I added lamely. 'And no one else had seen it.'

'And so you doubted the child's word?' He looked sorrowfully at me. If he had caught me robbing the church poor box I could not have felt more guilty.

'There are some things,' he continued gently, 'which are made manifest to children and to those of simple mind, and not to others. This may be one of those things, perhaps.'

He turned towards the door.

'I shall go straight to Henry's,' he said. 'He will know all about white robins, I've no doubt. What an excitement for the village, Miss Read! We are wonderfully blessed.'

His parting smile forgave me, and this particular Doubting Thomas returned to face an uproarious class.

By my desk stood Helen Coggs.

'I told you I sin 'un!' she said reproachfully.

CHAPTER 2

The Odd Man Out

By the time the news of our rare visitor had gone round the village, Fairacre School had broken up, and I was as free as my pupils to enjoy all the pleasures of summer.

I had a week at home before setting off for a fortnight's holiday with a friend in Yorkshire, and naturally kept an eye open for the white robin during that time. But I was unlucky.

Birds in plenty visited the bird table, including robins. At this stage of the year most of them looked harassed and shabby. All the hours of daylight were spent in flying to and fro in a ceaseless search for food for their clamouring babies.

On one occasion only did I see a baby robin, paler than its agitated father certainly, but nowhere near being albino. It emerged from the box hedge in my garden, its mottled breast gleaming in the sunlight, its wings trembling with anxiety for food. Snatching some crumbs from the bird table, the adult robin bustled back to the bold child which had followed him, and appeared to hustle it away into the protection of the hedge. I saw it no more.

I ventured quietly several times into the weedy haunt where the albino robin had been seen, and scratched my legs on the vicious brambles abounding there as I strained to see over the mossy wall into the vicarage garden. But again, I was unlucky.

The day before I was due to go away, I walked along the village street to the Post Office. Just emerging into the sunshine were Henry Mawne and a small boy.

'This is my great-nephew, Simon,' said Henry, introducing us. 'Say "How do you do" to Miss Read.'

'Hello,' said Simon, looking acutely embarrassed.

He was a very fair child with silky, almost white, hair, and startingly blue eyes. I judged him to be about seven or eight, and definitely underweight.

'Are you staying here long?' I asked him.

He looked anxiously at Henry Mawne.

'Possibly for a fortnight,' Henry answered for him. He began to fish in his pocket and produced a crumpled pound note.

'Hop back and get me a packet of foolscap envelopes from Mr Lamb,' he said to the boy. 'I forgot them when we were in the Post Office.'

The child vanished, and Henry Mawne spoke rapidly.

'He's my nephew's boy, and my godson. Trouble at home at the moment. His poor mother's very highly strung, and has just had another attack. Under hospital treatment at the moment, and my nephew is beside himself. We thought it would be a good thing for everyone concerned to have the boy down here for a time. Difficult for us though. We're too old to have children round us, and he's not an easy child, I must admit. Precocious in some ways, and a baby in others.'

'If he's still with you when I get back,' I said, 'bring him to tea. And if you want some books for him, the schoolhouse shelves are bulging with them.'

'Most kind, most kind! Ah, here he is!'

The child handed over the envelopes and change solemnly.

'Well, enjoy your break, Miss Read. No sign of the robin, I suppose?'

'Not yet. I'm living in hope though.'

We made our farewells, and Simon gave me a dazzling smile on parting.

There was no doubt about it. Simon might be pale and skinny, but he was a very handsome little boy.

I arrived back from my Yorkshire holiday on a fine August afternoon.

Driving south I noticed the farmers busy in the harvest fields, and when I reached home Mr Roberts was already combining the great field which lies beyond my hawthorn hedge.

The air was filled with the clatter and throb of machinery as the monster skirted my boundary, and then faded to a constant thrumming as it chugged into the distance.

Mrs Pringle, the school cleaner, was in my kitchen. She 'puts me straight', as she terms it, once a week, and despite her glum disposition which at times infuriates me, I welcome her ministrations, if not her comments, on my abode.

'Had a good time?' she enquired.

'Perfect!'

'Some people are lucky! I could do with a break myself, but a chance'd be a fine thing.'

'I'll put on the kettle,' I said diplomatically, 'I'm sure you need a cup of tea, and I certainly do.'

'It wouldn't come amiss,' she agreed, wringing out a wet duster. She sounded somewhat mollified, and her next remark sounded positively enthusiastic.

'You missed something this afternoon.'

'What was that?'

It was obviously something pleasant from the clear satisfaction she showed in the fact that I had missed it.

'That funny robin! He come to the bird table not half an hour ago.'

'Really? How marvellous! You *were* lucky to see him. I haven't yet.'

Mrs Pringle tucked her chins against her throat with every appearance of pleasure.

'Well, I was always one for noticing things, and I'd put out the crumbs from your bread bin which you'd forgotten to scrub out before leaving. Seems he liked them, stale though they were.'

'What's he like?' I said, ignoring the slur on my slatternly ways. In any case, I am used to Mrs Pringle's comments on my housewifery.

Her normally dour countenance lit up.

'Oh, he's a pretty dear! He was perched on the table with the sun behind him, and he looked just like a fluffy snowball. Except for his red breast, of course. He's a real beauty, I can tell you!'

'Let's hope he comes back soon,' I said, making the tea. 'I believe robins like biscuit crumbs. And mealworms. But I don't think I can face handling those.'

'I'll get old Mr Potts, as lives next door to me, to bring up some. He uses 'em for fishing. Come to that, I could bring up some in a jar when I come up to scrub the school out.'

'Don't you mind messing about with maggots?'

Mrs Pringle stirred her tea briskly.

'I'd do *anything* for that robin,' she declared stoutly.

If Mrs Pringle felt such devotion, I thought, what must be the rest of Fairacre's reaction to our rare bird?

'Who else has seen it while I've been away?'

'Ah now, let me think!' Mrs Pringle put her cup down upon the saucer with much deliberation. Her mouth was pursed in concentration.

'There was Mrs Partridge,' she said at last. 'And Mr Willet who was hoeing the vicar's rosebed last week, He was dumbstruck, he told me. Said he'd seen a white blackbird over at Springbourne when he was a lad, but never a white robin! Of course, he didn't see it real *close*. Not like I did just now.'

Mrs Pringle looked smug.

'Anyone else? Any of the children? I hope they won't scare it.'

'Not as I've heard. But Mr Mawne has built a funny little house in the vicar's garden, all covered in branches and that, with a few spy holes to look out of. Got his camera in there, so they say.'

'A hide,' I said.

'No, his *camera*,' repeated Mrs Pringle.

I let it pass.

'He's going to write a bit for the *Caxley Chronicle* and wants a picture to go with it. He's a clever one, that Mr Mawne.'

'He is indeed. I hope he manages to get a photograph.'

'Well, if he does, I reckon we'll get plenty more wanting to take snaps of our robin. Bring plenty of visitors to Fairacre, that bird will, I shouldn't wonder.'

'I hope not,' I said. 'I'm beginning to think that the less said about it the better. We don't want strangers frightening it away.'

Mrs Pringle's neck began to flush and her four chins to wobble. I know the signs well. Mrs Pringle had taken umbrage.

'You asked me yourself to tell you about the bird,' she began. 'We can't expect to keep a thing like that secret, so it's no good getting hoity-toity about it.'

'Sorry, sorry!' I cried. 'You misunderstood me. Have another cup of tea.'

Mrs Pringle buttoned up her mouth and pushed her cup towards me. The gesture was conciliatory, but I could see that I was not forgiven.

Certainly the advent of this little albino robin was causing a surprising stir in Fairacre.

For instance, the village fête, usually held in the vicarage grounds on a Saturday in August, was shifted this year to the garden of Henry Mawne at the other end of Fairacre.

There was considerable discussion about this locally.

'It's Mr Mawne's doing,' said one inhabitant accusingly. 'Just because he's bird-barmy us has to keep out of the vicar's garden. All for a *bird*!'

Others defended the plan.

'It's the right thing to do!'

'This white bird's *special*. No point in frightening it off. Why, it might go to Beech Green! And who'd want that?'

'Anyway, it'll make a nice change to go to the Mawnes, and Mrs Mawne's doing the teas herself.'

'Bribery,' muttered the first speaker, but it was plain that she was in the minority. Ninety per cent of Fairacre's population were devotedly in favour of giving the white robin every chance of survival.

Henry Mawne called one morning to return a book he had borrowed. We sat on the garden seat and I begged to be told the latest news.

'As far as I can tell there are four young robins. The other three are of normal colouring.'

'And where is the nest?'

'Oh, without doubt, in the ivy on the wall! This brood will be the last this season, I'm sure. It really is most exciting! I have seen the albino about half a dozen times now, and have taken several snaps which I'm about to develop.'

I told him that Mrs Pringle had seen it, and also that I rather feared that the bird was too popular for its own safety.

He nodded thoughtfully.

'Firstly, it's the children who might frighten it,' he said at last, 'but I'm sure you will do all in your power to protect it when they return to school. It faces danger too from other birds, as well as from any madman with a gun.'

I reassured him.

'And how is Simon?' I asked, now that the question of children had cropped up. 'Is he still with you?'

'No, he's returned home. I was going to say, "thank goodness", but that sounds heartless.'

'Children can be exhausting. Even angelic ones.'

'Oh, Simon's no angel, I can assure you! But he's plenty of reason to be difficult.'

He paused for a moment, as if trying to decide whether to confide in me or not. The cat wandered up and began to weave about my legs. I scratched the tabby back near the tail, a ploy most cats enjoy, while the silence lengthened.

'The fact is,' exploded Henry at last, 'the boy is odd man out in his family! There are three much older than he is – all sturdy, dark-haired extroverts like their father, my nephew. Not a nerve in their bodies! Strong as horses, never ill, good at games, and work as well. All out in the world and thriving.'

'Much older than Simon then?'

'Yes, he was one of these little afterthoughts, and I don't know that he was particularly welcome. Teresa thought her family was off her hands, you see, and then Simon came along.'

'Is she fair like the little boy? I thought he was a very handsome child.'

'So's his mother. Yes, a very pretty girl with a mop of fair hair. You could quite see why David fell for her.'

He sighed.

'*Very* pretty,' he repeated, 'but quite unsuitable.'

'Why?'

'A bundle of nerves. Always imagining she has something the matter with her. The complete hypochondriac! You should see their medicine cabinet. Twice the size of normal, and crammed with dozens of patent medicines. It's a marvel to me that the children are as healthy as they are. Even Simon, who is so like her, is comparatively cheerful, though no doubt he'll get more morbid as he grows older.'

Henry sounded gloomy.

'There's no reason to suppose that,' I said comfortingly. 'Apart from being rather thin and pale, he looked pretty healthy to me.'

'He's very attached to his mother, and I don't think it is altogether a good thing. Especially at the moment.'

'Is she too possessive?'

'Far from it. If anything she tends to reject the child. To be honest, I think she resents any attention which is not aimed at herself. My poor nephew is having the hell of a time.'

'Has she seen her doctor?'

'Too often, to my way of thinking, and all he says is something about her age, and being patient, and adjusting to situations, and similar codswallop. Sometimes I wonder if she needs a job of work, something to take her mind off herself. Though I pity anyone who employs her.'

'She certainly sounds most unhappy.'

'So's my poor David! He has to shoulder all the burdens while she sulks in this nursing home.'

'So she is getting treatment?'

'Yes, and at vast expense. They say it's a nervous complaint that should respond to whatever they're doing to her. I only hope it does. David and Simon are having a pretty thin time of it. They have a girl there who keeps house in a sketchy sort of way, but it's all very unsatisfactory.'

He sighed again, and stood up.

'Well, I musn't burden you with my troubles. Simon took to you, incidentally. You should feel honoured. He doesn't like many people, poor child, and I'm afraid many people don't like him. He has a pretty quick temper, unlike the other three. As I said, he's the odd bird out in that family.'

'Like the albino,' I said to turn his mind to happier things.

At once his face cleared, and he smiled.

'Like the albino,' he agreed. 'What a comfort nature is! Always something there for consolation.'

A sentiment with which I heartily concurred.

The holiday weeks sped by far too rapidly, and I enjoyed myself picking and bottling fruit, making jam, taking geranium cuttings and tidying the garden. I also decorated the kitchen, and although the standard of workmanship was far below that of Mr Willet, our local handyman-sexton-school-caretaker – and general factotum to Fairacre,

I was pleased with the result. Even Mrs Pringle commented grudgingly that 'it must be cleaner'.

When people ask me, as they frequently do, what I find to do in the long holidays which form one of the more attractive aspects of my job, I answer with some asperity. I do as they do. I clean my house, attend to the garden, prepare for the winter, go shopping, visit the dentist, put my meagre financial affairs in order, and so on. Why people imagine that teachers fall immediately into a state of suspended animation the minute term ends, I cannot think, but it is an attitude of mind which one often encounters.

As well as my own personal activities during August, I tried to pull my weight socially, helping at the fête in Henry Mawne's garden, supplying a local fund-raiser with a mammoth tray of gingerbread, and dispensing hospitality to a number of friends who had been kind enough to invite me to their homes during the past term. My old friend Amy, who lives at the village o Bent some miles distant, was one of these, and I was surprised to hear that she already knew about our white robin.

'But there's no secret about it, is there?' she enquired. 'You can't keep such a phenomenon to yourselves, you know.'

'I suppose not. It's just that I tremble for the bird. Too much publicity could put it in peril.'

'Rubbish!' said Amy stoutly. 'A sturdy albino robin can stand up to any amount of publicity, I'm sure. Robins are tough birds. I can't see any robin – white or coloured – being pushed around.'

I only hoped she was right, for certainly the subject of our rarity was cropping up quite often in the course of conversation with friends and neighbours.

What struck me was the affection, one might almost say reverence, with which they spoke of it. Country people are not given to sentimentality over animals. At times I think they go the other way, but I realize that I am a soft-hearted woman, incapable of passing a poor flattened hare or a squashed hedgehog on the road, without a pang of pity.

Very few of us had yet had a glimpse of the albino bird, but we eagerly questioned those who had, and a number of people remembered other white birds of the past.

On the whole, the blackbirds were those chiefly recalled, and as Henry Mawne told us that this particular variety of birds made up almost thirty per cent of albinos, it was not surprising. Miss Clare, who used to teach the infants at Fairacre School, remembered one white blackbird who had become very tame and had enchanted the children of an earlier generation in the village, and Mrs Willet, who had been one of those children, also remembered it vividly.

'There's nothing prettier than a pure white bird,' she declared. 'That one was white as a lily. Made you think of churches and altar cloths and that,' she added, waxing poetical.

Was this, I wondered, the reason for the awe which our white robin was inspiring? Did we unconsciously

connect its albinism with holiness and purity? Whatever were the reasons for our interest, there was no doubt that we were all eager to see it, and to cherish it.

I was lucky. I did not have to wait long.

On the very last day of the holidays the early sunshine woke me. I sat up in bed, and looked into the branches of an ancient apple tree outside the bedroom window.

There, its tiny talons gripping a lichen-covered twig, sat the white robin. Its eyes were dark and shining against the white satin of its head. The breast was still more orange than red, and glowed against its snowy plumage.

It was a breathtaking sight, and I did not dare to move. For a full half minute it sat there motionless, and then with a flash of white wings, it had gone.

Full of elation, I rose and dressed.

Now I was one of the élite who had actually seen the white robin!

CHAPTER 3

Snowboy

Term began, and in the usual flurry of settling the new babies in the infant class, and the young juniors in my own, there was little time to give to birdwatching.

Nevertheless, one or two of the children saw the robin, and we all learned a great deal from the long account of albinism in birds generally which Henry Mawne contributed to the *Caxley Chronicle*, complete with photographs taken from his hide in the vicar's garden.

To be honest, the photographs meant more to most of the *Caxley Chronicle*'s readers than Henry's somewhat erudite account of white birds. The early part of Henry's essay was devoted to genetic inheritance which successfully bogged down a number of readers anxious to assimilate the news of the robin rapidly, before passing on to the local football results.

For those still pursuing the subject of albinism there was a tricky passage involving the term NN, standing for the normal robin, and WW standing for the white variety. The offspring, wrote Henry, become NW, and as the albino gene is recessive further complicated combinations and permutations occur. As Mrs Pringle said: 'I didn't take in all that double-north and north-west stuff, but that Mr Mawne must have a good headpiece on him, that's for sure!'

She spoke for most of Fairacre.

As always when something unusual crops up, the subject of white birds occurred in various forms. There was a letter in *The Times* from a north country reader about a white blackbird which frequented his garden. To this Henry Mawne wrote a reply, and all Fairacre basked in the reflected glory when the letter was printed.

At much the same time, whilst I was reading that delightful book *The Country Diary of An Edwardian Lady*, I discovered that one of the January entries mentions 'a very curious Robin' which the author describes as light silvery grey and looking like a white bird with a scarlet breast when in flight. She comments truly, that 'it is a wonder it has not fallen a victim to somebody's gun'.

This fear, of course, was always with us, but we comforted ourselves with the thought that in such a small community as Fairacre we were united in wishing to protect our treasure. Certainly, if anyone were so wicked, or so foolhardy, as to raise a gun against our robin he would bring down the wrath of all upon his head. It would not take long to trace the culprit, that was sure.

That particular September the weather was warm. The low golden rays of the sun glinted upon the bales of corn waiting to be picked up and stacked in the barns. The streams of golden grain which had poured into the waiting wagons were now safely stored.

All the world seemed bathed in golden light. Yellow sunflowers and and golden rod in the cottage gardens added to this mellow warmth, and the first few falling leaves gleamed from the ground, awaiting the showers of bronze and gold which would join them later.

The dew was heavy each morning, and the children found mushrooms and early blackberries. In the gardens of Fairacre a bumper crop of plums weighed down the trees: round yellow gage plums dripping with sweetness, the old-fashioned golden drop plums so much prized by the jam-makers and, best of all, the enormous Victorias still awaiting a few days more in the sunshine to reach perfection.

There were plums everywhere. Baskets of plums were carried to neighbours. Bowls of plums stood on kitchen dressers. Bottles of plums gleamed like jewels from kitchen shelves. Jars of plum jam, plum jelly, plum chutney and plum preserves of all kinds jostled each other in kitchen cupboards.

Plums dominated the side desk in the schoolroom where the children left their elevenses. Usually, a few packets of biscuits or crisps, perhaps an apple or a banana, were to be seen but during the plum season the appearance of the ancient long desk was transformed by the local crop, now forming the main item of the dozen or so 'stay-bits', as the old people termed the snacks.

It was a lovely time when Fairacre enjoyed the fruits of its labours. Runner beans were being stuffed into freezers. Great bronze onions hung in ropes from out-house beams, and bunches of drying herbs from kitchen ceilings.

Marrows swayed in nets, like drunken sailors in hammocks. Potatoes rumbled into sacks, and apples were carefully wrapped in quarter sheets of the *Caxley Chronicle* and put to bed in rows in slatted boxes.

Housewives were red-eyed from peeling and pickling shallots, and their fingers appallingly stained by the constant handling of crops.

But who cared? This, for us country dwellers, was the crown of the year. We rejoiced in this plenty, and faced the coming winter with serenity, secure in the knowledge of our squirrels' hoards.

Harvest festival, as usual, found our parish church more crowded than at any other service in the year.

Perhaps country people are more conscious of the need for thanksgiving than their town cousins when the crops have been safely gathered in. Certainly the old familiar hymns from *Hymns Ancient and Modern* were sung lustily and sincerely, as our eyes roved over the bounties of the earth displayed in St Patrick's.

The children had contributed to this handiwork, as they had each year for generations. Each pew end bore a bunch of ears of corn, looped by a length of green knitting wool from the needlework cupboard. The base of the font was beautified by a garland of scrubbed carrots alternating with well polished apples. Giant marrows, dark green, pale green, and striped like tigers, were propped up in the porch for all to admire as the worshippers wiped their Sunday shoes on the mat.

The pulpit, the altar, and the steps to the chancel were left to the ladies of the parish to decorate, and a splendid job they made of it. Some said that their efforts were almost too artistic, and that feelings ran high when they were asked to incorporate six large loaves, contributed by the local baker, into their floral scheme.

Mr Partridge, with his usual pastoral tact, managed to calm the ladies' outraged feelings, and the loaves were removed from the delicate arrangements of wild bryony and sprays of bramble to a more suitable setting against the oak of the rood screen where they stood in a sturdy row and were much admired by those in the front pews.

'I very near broke a piece off one of they,' said our oldest shepherd. 'With a bit of tasty cheese that'd have passed the time lovely during parson's sermon.'

But temptation was resisted, and as always, the good things were gathered up after Harvest Festival Sunday and taken to Caxley Cottage Hospital for the patients' delectation.

'When I was in there one Michaelmas,' recalled the same old shepherd, 'we had marrer and marrer till it come out of our ears. We was right glad to get back to tinned peas again, I can tell you.'

Mrs Pringle, true to her word, had prevailed upon her neighbour, Mr Potts the fisherman, to provide her with some mealworms for the robin.

She brought them on the first occasion in a round plastic box which had once held margarine.

'There!' she said, whipping off the lid and displaying the revolting wriggling mass under my nose. 'Lovely, ain't they? They should bring the little old boy along.'

She put the open box on the asphalt part of the playground, in full view of the children in the classroom. As the weather was so warm, the door was propped open and there was every chance of someone seeing the robin if it appeared.

Frankly, I was doubtful. It was some weeks since I had enjoyed that breathtaking glimpse, although other robins had come to collect crumbs from my bird table as usual. Nevertheless, the mealworms were duly left in the strategic position selected, and we all waited for results.

We did not have long to wait. A gust of wind tipped over the light container and whipped it towards the school, spreading a trail of squirming maggots in its path.

'It's blown away!'

'It's gorn!'

'Them worms is runnin' away!'

'We've lost 'em!'

'Get 'em quick!'

'You get 'em! I can't touch 'em!'

There was instant pandemonium, and a concerted rush to rescue the mealworms.

'One of you hold the box,' I ordered, 'while the rest of you collect the worms. I'll go and fetch a heavier box for them.'

I hurried across to my kitchen, secretly thankful to be absent from maggot-collecting, and unearthed an ancient china pot which had once held *Gentleman's Relish*. It had a fine heavy base and was just deep enough to hold the robins' treat.

The children greeted it with rapture. The maggots were tipped in whilst I averted my gaze, and peace was restored.

There must have been one or two robins watching these proceedings from hiding places in the hedges for within a few minutes a pair came to snatch our largesse. But, to our disappointment, the white one did not appear.

'He'll come one day soon, you'll see,' Mrs Pringle assured the children when they told her of that morning's adventure. 'If I brings them worms regular, you won't have to wait long. You mark my words.'

The *Gentleman's Relish* jar was approved by the lady, and after that was in daily use.

'If I was you,' said Mrs Pringle, 'I'd have some of these nice maggots on your bird table. After all, that's where you saw him once, and maybe he's too timid to come into the open, seeing he's so conspicuous. You try it, Miss Read.'

Averse though I was to handling the things, I could see the sense of Mrs Pringle's argument, and I was also so eager to woo the robin to our territory that I braced myself to shake a few mealworms on to the bird table each day, shuddering the while.

There was no doubt about it, robins adored them. I only saw one robin at a time actually on the table, although I felt fairly sure that the pair which frequented the jar in the playground both came separately to my garden. I became convinced that they had nested somewhere in one of my hedges and that some of the young robins, now to be seen about, were their offspring.

I had no means of telling if other robins from the vicarage garden also came to get the mealworms from my table, but I suspected that they did. They must have watched very sharply for there were no fights. Any outsiders were careful to come when the coast was clear, so that there were no squabbles over territory, as often happens.

As the weather grew colder, more and more birds sought out the scraps provided, both on my garden bird table, and in the playground. They seemed to come in groups. A blue tit would appear, followed by half a dozen more. Then the chaffinches would sense that here was food to be had, and the blackbirds and always, of course, the ubiquitous sparrows and starlings.

They would make a concerted rush upon the food available, and then something would startle them and the bird table would be empty in a flash of wings. It was after just such a sudden exodus when I was turning away from the window that the white robin came again.

With his matchstick legs askew, and his liquid dark

eyes cocked upon the bounty, he was poised there for a full minute pecking at the scraps which he now enjoyed alone. His orange breast glowed like embers against the snowy feathers. He was even more handsome than on his first appearance.

And he was bolder. He must have glimpsed a movement

of mine, for he hopped about to face me, head still cocked, but picked up a maggot without undue hurry and flew off with it in the direction of the vicar's garden.

Later, that same day, the children saw him come to the mealworms in the playground, select a fine specimen, and depart.

It certainly looked as though Mrs Pringle's prognostications were correct.

By the time term ended, the white robin had become a frequent visitor to both my bird table and the playground, although he always chose to come when there were no other birds about.

He was now affectionately termed Snowboy, Snowball, Snowflake, Whitey, or Robbie by the children, and I had no fears that they would frighten the bird.

They treated it with devotion and deference. For them, and for the majority of Fairacre folk, the coming of this beautiful bird was a little miracle, and when school broke up for the Christmas holidays, I had to promise to cherish 'our Snowboy' on their behalf.

The congregation in St Patrick's Church on Christmas morning was not as large as that which gathered for Harvest Festival, but was certainly bigger than usual.

Many of the housewives were at home supervising the Christmas dinner, but there was a fair sprinkling of visitors to engage our attention, and plenty of new gloves and scarves to admire which had obviously been acquired that morning.

The flowers and evergreens caught our eye. Christmas roses, late chrysanthemums, trails of shiny ivy leaves, holly and mistletoe wreathed the font and pulpit, and two splendid poinsettias flanked the altar.

What with all this excitement, and the thought of presents at home and the feasting to come, it was hardly surprising that the choirboys went a trifle flat. Mr Annett, as organist, thumped out the Christmas hymns in as staccato a manner as was humanly possible, in an effort to quicken the pace, but he might just as well have spared himself.

Fairacre boys, as I know to my cost, 'will not be druv', and they lagged half a bar behind and were blissfully unaware of their choirmaster's rising blood pressure.

I was interested to see my young friend Simon again, standing in the Mawnes' pew and flanked by his dark-haired father, whom I knew slightly, and a pretty fair-haired woman who was obviously Teresa, his mother.

She was tall and slim, wrapped in a short chinchilla coat. She did not join in the singing, but stared straight ahead, ignoring the sidelong glances which both Henry Mawne and her husband David occasionally cast in her direction.

The party came out of church fairly quickly, so that I was able to observe Simon's mother as she came up the aisle.

She was exceptionally pretty, but her face was pale and expressionless. It was the brilliance of her eyes which struck me. They were large and of that intense pale blue which is sometimes seen in fanatics. Garibaldi, they say, had just such eyes, and so too have several unbalanced criminals.

I felt a quiver of fear as my gaze met hers for one fleeting moment. Here, I was sure, was someone desperately unhappy, and potentially dangerous too.

Poor woman! Poor David! But most of all, poor young Simon, I thought, watching his fair head, level with the beautiful grey fur coat, as he followed his mother into the winter sunshine.

CHAPTER 4

Bitter Weather

The worst of the winter weather came, as usual, after Christmas. Heavy snow towards the end of January kept a few of the children at home for a day or two, and those that did arrive frequently had coughs or head colds.

So many of the mothers were out at work that I sometimes wondered if a few of the children were sent off to school when they would have been better off at home in the early stages of a cold. In former times, there would probably have been a granny sitting by the fire, or a single aunt who would have been free, and more than willing to care for a sickly child, until its mother came home, but grannies and single aunts also went to work these days, and children had to learn to stand on their own feet rather earlier than my own generation did.

All that I could do was to ensure that the stoves were kept banked up, although there was considerable opposition to this, of course, from Mrs Pringle. I heated the children's milk too, for those who could not face a bottle with flakes of ice at the top, and stirred in a spoonful of drinking chocolate from my store cupboard, if they liked it.

At least most of them were warmly clad these days. Even the Coggs children had wellington boots, and some shabby slippers to change into when they arrived. And, while the weather was at its most bitter, I relaxed my stern rule about everyone playing outside for the full quarter of an hour at break time, and let them cluster round the tortoise stove for half the appointed time.

Snow always brings out the worst in Mrs Pringle. She looks upon it as a personal enemy, a despoiler of clean floors, a hazard to life and limb, and the unnecessary salt rubbed into the wounds of everyday living.

'It isn't as though I was getting any younger,' she grumbled to me after the children had been buttoned up, gloved and scarved, and sent on their way.

'It's this weather as makes my leg flare up,' she continued. 'I don't say nothing about it in the ordinary way, as well you know, Miss Read.'

This was news to me, but I forbore to comment. Experience has taught me to let Mrs Pringle have her head when she is indulging in personal martyrdom.

'But all this extra work Takes Its Toll, as they say. That lobby needs a good scrub out every evening, and I can't do it. As for sacks, I'm down to my last two. I did ask Mr Roberts if he'd got any to spare, but they're all these useless plastic things these days that don't sop up nothing.'

'We could wipe them,' I suggested.

'*Wipe them?*' boomed Mrs Pringle, turning red in the face. 'What good would that do? Might just as well wipe the floor itself while I was at it!'

'Of course, of course!' I said hastily.

'No, I sometimes wonder if the folk who live abroad aren't best off. Take my cousin's boy. He's in South Africa, and she had a letter last week to say he was sunbathing. *Sunbathing*, mark you! In January!'

'Lucky chap,' I said.

'Well,' said the lady, heaving herself to her feet from the desk top where she had been seated. 'This won't buy the baby a new frock. One thing I know, if I win the pools one day I'll spend the winter in South Africa.'

One good thing about the cold spell was that the birds, including Snowboy, came much more boldly for the food we put out.

Even the rooks came down into the playground for our largesse, and one, bolder than the rest, took to balancing precariously on the bird table, much to the annoyance of the smaller birds.

There was no doubt that the coming of Snowboy-Snowball-Snowflake-etc. had created much more interest in birds generally in the village, and when we heard that Henry Mawne had been invited to appear on local television and to show some of his film on the albino robin, we were heady with pride.

'Henry will be on soon after six o'clock on Thursday,'

the vicar told me, 'and if you would care to come and see him on our set, my wife and I would be delighted.'

As the vicar has a colour television I accepted gratefully.

'Watch out for Thursday soon after six!' shouted Mr Lamb from the Post Office, when he caught sight of me at the post-box on the wall of his abode.

'Don't forget Mr Mawne's on on Thursday,' warned Mrs Pringle.

We all reminded each other when we met. It was quite apparent that everyone in Fairacre would be watching on the great day.

The *Caxley Chronicle* carried a reminder to its readers on the front page, and was careful to point out that Henry Mawne was one of its distinguished contributors. Side by side with this pleasurable announcement, was the un- welcome news that the price of this valuable journal would be going up by one penny at the next issue. I felt that the editor and staff could not have chosen a better time to make the announcement. Henry Mawne's fame sugared the pill very nicely.

On Thursday evening, I presented myself at the vicarage, and found several other friends there. With glasses of sherry in our hands, we stared at the screen awaiting Fairacre's great moment.

I must say that Henry looked extremely elegant and unusually tidy in the studio. The make-up department seemed to have smoothed over most of his wrinkles, and given him a healthy flush, although the heat from the lights or general excitement might have accounted for his robust look. He was wearing his best hacking jacket and his National Trust tie, and we all agreed that he was a worthy representative of the village.

But naturally enough, the white robin eclipsed him in splendour. About a dozen slides were shown, for the first time, and we sat entranced at the bird's beauty. Henry had certainly managed to get some superb pictures, and when the allotted ten minutes were over, and the screen filled with an appalling picture of a head-on crash, police cars, and ambulances with doors yawning as stretchers were being inserted, we watched the vicar switch off, with relief, and lived once again our splendid distinction on television.

It was the next evening when my old friend Amy drove over from Bent.

Amy and I were at college together many years ago, and although she is married, much travelled, always exquisitely dressed and wealthy, in complete contrast to me, we have a great deal in common, and the bond of friendship grows stronger with the years.

She has a tiresome habit of trying to reform me, and another, equally annoying, of trying to find me a husband. Luckily, as the years go by, the chances of this being accomplished grow slighter, and Amy's efforts are less wholehearted, much to my relief.

'My dear Amy,' I have said to her on many occasions, 'you must know, surely, that some people are the marrying sort and some are not. I'm one of the latter, so do stop beating your head against a brick wall. I am perfectly happy as I am.'

I am not sure that Amy really believes me, but she is gradually coming round to the idea that I do not sob myself to sleep each night because I am unwed.

Of course we discussed the programme. In contrast to all Fairacre's enthusiasm, Amy was somewhat cool.

'Personally, I question that bird being an albino,' she said. 'I always understood that a *pure* albino bird had pink eyes and no colour in its legs and so on.'

'Well, it's albino enough for most of us,' I said stoutly. 'And come to think of it, I believe Henry did say something on that point.'

'Not enough. In a brief programme like that he should have been *much* more precise. I've no doubt that he will get plenty of criticism from true ornithologists.'

'But Henry *is* a true ornithologist!' I cried, 'You really are a carping old horror, Amy!'

She began to laugh.

'And you and the rest of the Fairacre folk are absolutely besotted with that blighted bird! But I readily admit that it's a beauty, and I can't say fairer than that, can I?'

'Have a glass of sherry,' I said, forgiving her. 'And tell me all the latest news.'

'You haven't, by any chance, a drier sherry than that, have you?' enquired Amy, watching me pour out a fine tawny glassful.

'Sorry, no! I won this at the summer fête.'

Amy shuddered.

'It's jolly good. Rather like that raisin wine we used to buy in Cambridge at three and six a bottle in the old days. But if you don't like it you can have Robinson's lemon barley water instead.'

'I'm sure this will be delicious,' said Amy, lying bravely, as she accepted the glass.

'What news of Vanessa?' Amy's attractive niece is a great favourite of mine. Now that she is married and lives in a castle in Scotland, I do not see much of her, but we keep in touch.

'Thriving, I'm glad to say. Both children doing well, and I believe she is already planning for a third.'

'Good heavens! Does she really want *three*?'

'She wants *six*, so she says. Personally, I consider it rather selfish, but of course there's much more room in Scotland, and you could lose six children in that barn of a castle without missing them for a fortnight.'

'Well, all I can say is, I admire her pluck. Of course, young things can plan families so much more easily these days, can't they?'

'You shouldn't know anything about it.' said Amy severely, 'as a respectable spinster.'

'You and Lady Bracknell,' I replied, 'would make a good pair. She didn't believe in tampering with natural ignorance either.'

Amy put down her glass.

'Talking of marriage, would you like to meet our new organist at Bent?'

'I don't mind meeting the new organist, but I warn you that I shan't have marriage in mind.'

'I'm having a little dinner party next week. Do come. The poor fellow knows no one locally, and is in rather wretched digs. I don't think he gets enough to eat. James said he'd be home, and said you must come, as he is so fond of you.'

'Don't flatter me, Amy dear. Of course, I'll come, and I shall look forward to seeing your attractive husband, and the new organist. What's his name?'

'Unfortunately, it's Horace Umbleditch. Quite tricky to say when one is making introductions. But he's quite a charmer, and has a most elegant figure. James said: "Fatten him up, but don't marry him off!" At times, James is a trifle coarse.'

'James is a sensible man,' I told her. 'More sherry?'

'Do you know, I think I will. It's rather like a blend of good quality cough linctus and elderberry wine. It's growing on me.'

'Well, keep yourself in hand. It's no use becoming addicted to the stuff. This is all I've got.'

I filled her glass again, while Amy enlarged on the guests whom I should meet at the proposed party, and I looked forward even more eagerly to my evening out.

The weather continued to be cold and miserable. Although most of the snow had cleared, there were still white patches under the hedges and on the northerly slopes which the sun did not reach.

'It's waiting for more to come,' said Mr Willet gloomily, surveying the dark corner by the vicar's wall. Here, in the cold shade, slivers of snow lay under the bushes, undisturbed by the children. In this weather they rushed to the nearby lavatories, and back again, at record speed, thankful to regain the shelter of the schoolroom and the comfort of the ancient tortoise stoves.

As usual, Mr Willet was right. I would back his judgement about our weather against any professional weatherman in the country. In the last week of term, the skies grew ominously overcast, and one night the snow fell from ten o'clock until six in the morning. Once again the lanes of Fairacre were white. The fields glistened beneath their blanket of snow, dazzling against the dark clouds above them.

The bare black trees and hedges made the whole scene look like a stark charcoal drawing. It hurt one's eyes to look for long. One craved for a splash of colour to warm the bleak outlook.

'You'd think by March,' said Mr Willet, 'that we'd see a bit of sun. Dear knows what's gone amiss with spring these days! Why, when I was a boy we reckoned to pick primroses and violets in March. Not much chance of that this year.'

He watched me scattering crumbs for the birds.

'Poor things! No weather for the young 'uns. Seen anything of our robin?'

'He comes most days. He's looking marvellous, and I believe he's made a nest in my garden somewhere.'

'Has he now? You watch out that cat of yours don't get the young 'uns. Be a bit of all right if they turned out white, wouldn't it?'

Ernest and Patrick had wandered up and were listening

to our conversation. They took up the theme with enthusiasm.

'How many eggs do robins lay?'

I offered them what scanty knowledge I had gleaned from the bird book on my shelf.

'About half a dozen, I think,' I hazarded.

'Then we might get six new white ones!' cried Patrick. He grabbed at a passing infant who had just arrived. 'Here that, fatty? We might get lots more Snowballs this spring.'

'Run inside,' I said to the children. 'I'm just coming, and it's far too cold to stay outdoors.'

'Well, I hope the boy's right,' said Mr Willet, preparing to set off to his home. 'Be a fine thing if we had a few more white 'uns.'

'I've a feeling it doesn't work that way,' I replied. 'Didn't Mr Mawne's article say something about missing a generation? I must look it up.'

'If it was that bit about the Ns and Ws, I was fair flummoxed,' admitted Mr Willet. 'I was out of my depth after two lines of that, but I do remember there was a bit of doubt about it.'

'I'll ask Mr Mawne when I see him,' I promised.

'That'll be some time. He's off on one of these cruises. Gone to Crete, I believe, on a boat with a lot of other bird people. He's lecturing them, so Mrs Mawne told me.'

'Has she gone too?'

'No, she said she had quite enough of birds in Fairacre without going overseas to see a lot more.'

'She would have missed this beastly cold spring,' I said.

'Ah well! Maybe it'll all be over before you break up. Think of that! You'll have your deck chair up before the month's out!'

'That'll be the day,' I said, folding my coat more tightly about me.

And picking my way through the slushy playground, I went into the school to face my duties.

CHAPTER 5

A Nest of Robins

I spent a considerable time getting ready for Amy's dinner party, and wished I had asked her the usual question, 'Long or short skirt?', when I had been invited. As it was, I had left this vital question too late to bother her, and weighed up the pros and cons for the umpteenth time.

In this bitter weather a long skirt could be a great comfort. On the other hand, it was the devil to drive in, and in Amy's well-heated house it might well prove too warm. It must be admitted though, that if one wished to honour one's hostess, a long skirt looked as though one had really made some effort.

But then again, one did not want to appear over-dressed, and it seemed that short skirts were in again for evening occasions. Also I had recently bought a stunning silk shirt-waister which Amy had not yet seen, and I was strongly inclined to put it on. After a good deal of shilly-shallying I decided to wear the latter, and if every other woman was sweeping around in floor length kaftans and black velvet skirts, good luck to them!

One of the comforts of middle age, I find, is the comparative peace of mind which engulfs one when one has finally decided what to put on. When young, one's evening can be ruined by the thought that one's shoes are the wrong colour, or one's hair needs shampooing. Advancing age has its modest compensations.

The night was clear and frosty. Some snow still lay along the edges of the road and covered the sloping banks which faced north. The car's headlights made dark tunnels of the trees ahead on my way to Bent, and there were few wayfarers about in the winter cold.

Amy's house was as warm and welcoming as her greeting. Great mop-headed chrysanthemums graced the hall table, and two bowls of shell-pink Lady Derby hyacinths scented her drawing-room. Mine, needless to say, had hardly put their noses through the fibre.

Horace Umbleditch proved to be an elegant man with dark hair and a gold-rimmed monocle swinging on a black silk cord about his neck. From Amy's description I had expected a somewhat pathetic figure, undernourished and shy, but the new organist, although enviably slim, was obviously fit and distinctly voluble. I could see that he would more than hold his own in the assembled company.

James, Amy's husband, enveloped me in a bear's hug, kissed me on both cheeks, and held me at arm's length to admire my new silk frock. One can quite see why James is so attractive to the opposite sex. I am not very susceptible, but even my elderly spinster's heart melts when I meet James. He looks at you very closely, as though you were the only woman he was waiting to see. I think it is because he is short-sighted, and he is far too vain to wear spectacles, but the result is the same, and very pleasurable it is. Knowing James, I forgive all – and there is plenty to forgive – but I adore him.

There were ten of us at dinner, mostly Bent friends, some of whom I had met before. I was interested to see that short skirts outnumbered long by three to two. The vicar's wife sported a long black one, made of such heavy ribbed silk that I longed to stroke it, and the youngest wife present wore a dashing spotted affair with frills reaching to the ground.

As always, Amy's food was delicious. A creamy fish dish, sizzling in our ten ramekins, was followed by pheasant, then lemon sorbet or apple and blackberry tart, and a superb dessert of black and white grapes, pears and peaches.

'Coffee in the drawing-room,' Amy called to me as I went upstairs. I always relish Amy's bathroom. It is a symphony of primrose yellow and deep gold. Even the soap echoes the colour scheme, and best of all, the towels intended for visitors' use are clearly labelled GUEST. How often, in less elegantly appointed bathrooms, I have wondered whether to wipe my wet hands on a corner of my hostess's – or possibly host's – towel, or use the foot mat. It is plain sailing if there is one of those little huckaback items, embroidered with a lady in a crinoline standing by some knot-stitch hollyhocks, but distinctly daunting if one is confronted by six equally sized towels shoulder-to-shoulder on the towel rail.

Horace Umbleditch brought my coffee and sat beside me.

'Amy has been telling me about your famous Fairacre robin. I'm particularly interested as I know Henry Mawne's nephew slightly.'

'David?'

'That's right. My sister is a neighbour of theirs, and occasionally sits in for young Simon if they are going out. She had heard about the robin from them, of course.'

'It's a terrific thrill for us. So far the robin has thrived. We're hoping there will be more one day.'

'Simon's much impressed, I gather from my sister. She sees quite a bit of the boy. She trained as a Norland nurse and has a very soft spot for young Simon. His mother has been ill, as no doubt you know.'

I said that I did.

'There's some talk of the boy going to boarding school next September. A good thing, I should think. Teresa gets no better, and it's affecting Simon badly. I know my sister worries a lot about the family.'

'They are lucky to have such an understanding neighbour.'

'Well, it works both ways. They have always been good to Irene on the rare occasions when she has been ill. Thank God we're a hardy family, and don't ail much.'

Amy bore down upon us at this juncture and carried Horace off to talk to the young wife in the spotted skirt.

As James took his place, I was well content, but I pondered on this comment on Teresa Mawne as I drove home under a starlit sky, and was considerably disturbed. The memory of that blank, blue, fanatical stare was fresh in my mind, and I trembled for those who lived with it.

It was during the last few days of term that I caught a glimpse of the white robin in my garden. To my joy, he was feeding a normal coloured robin, presumably a female, who was quivering her wings and obviously begging for food.

Was this his mate? Would we soon see some young robins? I put these questions to Henry Mawne as soon as he returned from his tour of Crete.

He was looking remarkably hale, with a splendid sun-tan which contrasted noticeably with the pinched blue complexions of the rest of us Fairacre folk.

'Almost certainly his mate,' he said. 'And I've no doubt you'll soon hear the young birds somewhere in that hedge of yours. But don't expect any white ones. I told you all about that.'

I hardly liked to say that I had not quite taken in this important fact, but Henry guessed.

'I suppose you, and all those silly children, and everyone else in the village for that matter, expects half a dozen snow-white robins this spring.'

'Well –' I began diffidently.

'I don't know why I bother to explain these simple facts, I really don't. Did you read my article?'

'Yes, I did.'

'I made it quite plain, I thought, that the *children* of an albino would be normal in colouring. It is *just possible* that an albino might occur in the grandchildren. And then probably only one in four.'

'Thank you for explaining,' I said humbly.

'So do spread the word, Miss Read, that we shall not see any more white robins this spring.'

'I will. But we might see one, say, next year?'

Henry Mawne looked severe.

'That's looking rather far ahead. Anything might happen to this year's brood. I shouldn't like to say that we should see a white one *next* year even. Too many hazards. Your cat for one.'

This wholly unjustified attack on poor Tibby, not even present to defend himself, quite took my breath away.

Seeing his advantage, Henry walked away briskly before I had time to answer.

Easter fell early in April, and although the weather over that weekend remained overcast and chilly, the wind changed towards the end of the week, and welcome sunshine flooded the countryside.

It was wonderful, after such a long bleak spell, to wake to warmth and gentle breezes. The crocuses burst into bloom. The daffodil buds seemed to shoot an inch higher overnight, and in all the cottage gardens hoeing, raking and digging began with renewed hope.

Joseph Coggs appeared on my doorstep and offered his services as assistant gardener. I gladly accepted.

Mrs Coggs was out at work, I knew. The twins were looked after, somewhat sketchily, by a neighbour who had children of the same age. The youngest pair were taken with Mrs Coggs to work at the various establishments in the village where she was employed as a daily help.

Joseph was the odd man out, and I was glad to have him safely with me, and to enjoy his company at my lunchtime. He seemed happy to come and make himself useful, and certainly appreciated my cooking. He was observant, and unusually knowledgeable about natural life.

I watched him staring at a worm which was wriggling purposefully towards a damp garden bed. He accepted a mug of coffee without shifting his gaze.

'Them 'as got eight hearts,' he informed me.

'Really?'

'And you chop 'em in half and they makes two worms.'

'I hope you're not going to try it.'

'Course not!' he sounded affronted.

'What are you going to do when you grow up, Joe?'

I thought of his drunken father. Not much of an example there for a young boy.

'I be goin' to be a gamekeeper. Like my grandpa was.'

'I think you would be good at that.'

'And you gets a new suit every two years. And real leather boots. Proper tweed the suit is. My grandpa told me.'

'And where did he work?'

Joseph looked nonplussed.

'A good way off. For some Lord Somebody. Might have been Aylesbury or round there. My grandpa liked him, and this Lord Whoever give him a watch when he was an old man.'

Joseph is not usually so forthcoming, and I was interested to learn something of his background.

'Snowboy's been in and out the box hedge,' he said, handing over the empty mug. 'Shall us go and look?'

'No, no,' I said hastily. 'We mustn't disturb him. Do you think there's a nest there?'

'I bet she's sitting,' said Joseph, 'and Snowboy's taking in some grub for her. What we got today, miss?'

'Cottage pie, and apple fluff.'

'Smashing!' said my gardener, setting off to hoe with renewed energy.

Apart from a couple of days when I was out visiting, Joseph spent most of the hours of daylight with me. It seemed to suit Mrs Coggs, young Joe and me as well. He was no bother, happy and obedient, and opened my eyes to a number of things in the garden I had missed.

A blackbird had built in the crook of two branches in the hawthorn bush. Joseph spotted the nest in a trice, but was careful, I noticed, not to visit it too often.

'Four eggs,' he told me proudly.

'And down the field bank there's a wren nesting, but she's been too durned clever for me. Can't find it nohow, but I'll lay she've got more'n four.'

I quoted the old verse to him.

> The dove said: 'Coo,
> What shall I do?
> For I have *two*!'

'Pooh!' said the wren,
'I have *ten*
And bring them up
Like gentlemen!'

It appealed to the boy, and I had to repeat it several times until he had it by heart, I made a note to teach it to my class next term.

One morning of bright sunshine, I carried his mug out into the garden, but could not see him anywhere.

Then I became aware of a grubby hand beckoning me silently towards the box hedge at the farthest corner of the garden.

I approached warily, and with some feeling of annoyance. The boy had been told explicitly to keep well away from the white robin's possible nest. It would be infuriating if the parent birds were disturbed and deserted the nest.

'She'm off for a minute,' breathed Joseph. He was holding aside a sturdy branch. The boy's face was alight with wonder, and I had not the heart to chide him.

There, on the ground, in a mossy cup, lay five robin's eggs, white as pearls, and freckled with tiny pink spots. It was a sight to catch the breath.

'Cover it again,' I whispered, 'and come away.'

We crept quickly back to the garden seat near the house, and almost immediately a flash of white wings showed that Snowboy was returning to see if all was well with his wife and potential family.

'I wonder how many white 'uns among them five,' said Joseph, clutching his mug.

'None this year,' I said.

'Might be two or three,' continued Joseph, still bemused.

'Mr Mawne said we couldn't expect any white birds this year,' I said patiently.

Joseph took a long drink, wiped his mouth on the back of his hand, and settled back with a sigh.

'Wouldn't it be fine if us got FIVE?' he cried, eyes shining.

Against such touching faith I was powerless, and gave up.

CHAPTER 6

Our New Pupil

Term had begun when Henry Mawne rang me one evening.

He sounded unusually agitated, and so was I when he asked if he could call immediately about a pressing matter.

'Of course,' I said. 'Bring Elizabeth and I'll get some coffee ready. What's it about?'

'Oh, I couldn't possibly tell you on the telephone, and I won't bring my wife, though many thanks for inviting her. And please don't bother with coffee. I find it keeps me awake these nights. I'll be with you in half an hour or less.'

If there is anything I dislike it is suspense. Why on earth couldn't Henry have given me some clue? To say, in a somewhat shocked voice, that the subject was unsuitable for relaying over the telephone system, was to bring to mind the worst excesses known to man. What had Henry discovered in our midst? Murder, mayhem, illegitimacy, fraud, bigamy? My mind ranged over all as I tidied away piles of marking, and took out the dead flowers, which I had intended to remove throughout the evening.

It was too bad of Henry to keep me dangling like this, I thought, even if it were for only half an hour. I recalled the poor young wives in war time who were only told that their husbands were missing, and no further word was given to them, often for months or years. One in particular I remembered, who wailed tragically, saying: 'I'd sooner know Bob was *dead*, than not know *anything*!'

There had been looks of horror and disgust at this *cri de coeur*, but she had my entire sympathy.

By the time I had faced a raving lunatic at large in the village, various fatal accidents, unspecified incurable diseases with which the Mawnes had been afflicted and which involved asking me for advice, a court case against me for maltreating a child – a clear case here of guilty conscience, as I had administered a sharp slap to Patrick's leg when he had attempted to kick one of the infants – and a number of other unpleasant contingencies, the doorbell rang, and I hastened to admit my tormentor.

To my chagrin, he looked remarkably calm and happy, the maddening fellow.

'Do sit down,' I said, trying to appear equally at ease. 'Now how can I help?'

'It's about Simon,' he said, coming with admirable brevity to the nub of the matter. 'Trouble at home again.'

'I'm sorry to hear it.'

'Teresa's had a pretty frightening attack. David came home to find her tearing up everything she could lay hands on. Flowers, Simon's toys, David's books! Ghastly! The worst of it was that poor Simon couldn't get out of the room, and had to watch it all. David feels sure that she might have attacked the boy, if he hadn't arrived in time.'

'So what has happened to her?'

'She's back in the nursing home. I honestly don't know if it's the right place for her, but at least she's safe for the moment, and so are David and Simon. The thing is, we've offered to have the child again, and I wondered if you could possibly admit him to the school for an unspecified period?'

'No bother at all,' I assured him. 'We'd like to have him, and he knows some of the other children. He'll soon settle, I'm sure.'

Henry sighed gustily.

'Well, that's a relief. I promised David that I would speak to you and ring him tonight. How soon can he be admitted?'

'As soon as you like.'

Henry rose, and shook my hand warmly.

'I'm so very grateful. It will be a weight off David's mind. He's due to go to Holland on a business trip of some importance to the firm, and I hope he can still make it. This will help enormously.'

I accompanied him to the door. He was still profuse in his thanks.

I returned exhausted to the sitting-room, and collapsed upon the newly plumped cushions.

'Tibby,' I said to the cat, 'there's a lot to be said for casting your burdens, as long as you are not on the receiving end.'

Mrs Pringle's temper improved with the weather, I was thankful to note. She was even heard to sing, in a deep lowing contralto, as she washed up the dinner plates.

'Glad to see the back of that snow,' she admitted. 'Fair back-breaking work that makes. And I was thinking we could just about do without the stoves. Wicked to burn fuel when there's no need.'

'I think we'll see how we go until next week,' I said hastily. 'The wind is still quite sharp.'

'Well, we'll wait and see then,' said Mrs Pringle, with unusual docility. 'But the Office won't like it if we wants more coke this term.'

At that moment, the white robin flew down to the tin of mealworms, snatched up a beakful and flew off to my garden.

'The babies are hatched,' said Mrs Pringle.

'How d'you know?'

'I heard them.'

'Heard them? When?'

Mrs Pringle looked slightly abashed.

'Last evening. I come up with some fresh tea towels, and you was on the phone, otherwise I'd have knocked. I felt I must have a peep.'

'Oh, Mrs Pringle! And you know how we've threatened the children about frightening them!'

Mrs Pringle drew herself up huffily, and her face resumed its normal expression of dudgeon.

'Well, I never *looked*. Wasn't no need. Just as I was creeping up to the nest, old Snowboy flew in, and I could hear them youngsters twittering. Sweetly pretty it sounded, I can tell you.'

'That's marvellous news,' I cried, relief flooding me. 'I must let Mr Mawne know.'

'You needn't bother. I told him myself as I went back home,' said Mrs Pringle, sweeping out majestically.

How is it that that woman always has the last word?

Henry brought Simon to school on the following Monday morning.

The child looked peaky, with dark smudges under his eyes, but he seemed glad to be with us, and I put him to sit next to Ernest, who is a kindly child and enjoys looking after people and animals.

Henry was profuse in his thanks as I accompanied him into the lobby.

'I'm glad to have him,' I assured him. 'How is his mother?'

'Much the same. Elizabeth is visiting her today, and intends to give her news of Simon, but I doubt if she'll be interested. It's a difficult case. Even the doctors admit that, and heaven alone knows where it will all end.'

'Well, you can do no more than you are doing, and at

least you have the comfort of knowing she's in safe hands.'

'That's true, as far as it goes. But is *safety* enough? We all want to see her restored to normal mental health, with the usual maternal feelings, and pleasure in family life. But can this nursing home do that? That's what worries me. Are we any nearer curing mental illnesses than we were when the poor things were carted off to the local Bedlam?'

'Of course we are,' I said stoutly, trying to rally the unhappy man. 'I should think more advances have been made in that field than in any other. I'm sure you'll see progress in a week or two's time.'

Henry Mawne shook his head sadly, and made no reply, but clanked across the door scraper and set off towards home. Watching his departing figure, it occurred to me that my old friend had aged suddenly in the past few months, and I could only hope that Simon's mother would improve rapidly before the strain disrupted her family still further.

CHAPTER 7

A Tragedy

May arrived, serene and sunny. There were no 'rough winds to shake the darling buds', and the late narcissi and tulips stood up straight as soldiers in the sunshine.

The children came to school in summer frocks and tee-shirts. The stoves were empty, and polished to jet black for the summer season. Woe betide anyone dropping pencil parings or toffee papers behind the glossy bars of the fire guard! Mrs Pringle intended her handiwork to remain unsullied for several months. An occasional dusting, or a little light attention with dustpan and soft brush was all that should be needed now that her arch-enemy, the coke, was not in evidence.

There was plenty of activity in my box hedge. Snowboy and his mate flew in and out a hundred times a day, and the twittering grew stronger. We all resisted the temptation to peep, but Henry Mawne had a quick look, pronounced that there were definitely four babies, and that they would be out of the nest within the week.

He did not have time to dally on this occasion as he

was expecting a telephone call, but I went with him to the gate, and watched him enter the car.

'Any white ones?' I called.

'Of course not,' said Henry, quite snappily, and it dawned on me that probably everyone in Fairacre asked him the same question, despite his reiteration of the fact that we could not expect any albinos in this year's broods.

At the end of May we had our first view of the babies. They were fluttering after Snowboy in the empty playground, clamouring to be fed. I saw them from the schoolroom window, and debated whether I should let the children know the good news. I decided that I would risk opening the door very gently, so that the class could see the family at a distance.

They were so breathlessly quiet you could have heard the proverbial pin drop. One or two stood up at the back of the room to get a better view, but I was touched by their intent silence and look of wonder on their faces.

After a minute or two, the white robin fluttered away towards my garden, followed by his four vociferous youngsters. His anxious mate met him halfway, and together they shepherded their family towards their home.

Very gently I closed the door.

'Ain't that *nice*!' said Patrick with immense satisfaction.

There was a chorus of agreement, and then Eileen spoke.

'But no white ones.'

There was a general sigh.

'You'd think there'd be *one*!' said Ernest sadly.

'Well, you know what Mr Mawne told us,' I reminded them. 'We might get some next year.'

'My Uncle Henry,' said Simon, in his high polite voice which contrasted so noticeably with his companions' country burr, 'says he's bloody tired of trying to explain just that.'

We were all so taken aback at his casual use of a swear word that he went unreprimanded.

'Very understandable,' I said at last. 'Now take out your atlases, and turn to map eighteen.'

As the summer term progressed, I observed Simon with considerable interest.

He was certainly gaining strength, and seemed much more at ease, although he remained pale and did not seem to put on weight.

He seemed attached to Ernest, his desk mate, and Ernest obviously looked upon our visitor as his special charge, but the rest of the children did not seem to accept the boy completely. I put it down to inbred country suspicion of anything foreign, and realised that I could do little about it except to see that no antagonism was shown towards him.

In some ways Simon was admired. For one thing, he was always imaculately dressed, and his fair hair beautifully trimmed. Also he was quiet – almost laconic – in his conversations with his fellows. Only once did I see the flash of temper about which Henry Mawne had spoken. Someone knocked over his paint water, by accident, ruining his picture. Simon flew at the child, his eyes blazing, but luckily his victim had retreated rapidly and in good order, and nothing worse ensued.

He was also in some demand when it came to team games, for he had an unerring aim, and as a fielder could knock down a wicket at a considerable distance when we played our rudimentary cricket or rounders in Mr Roberts' field. The vicar had presented the school with a set of deck quoits some years earlier and at Simon's plea these were dug out of the cupboard and used at playtime. The base was set up some distance from the birds' mealworm tin, a chalk line drawn for the competitors, and this game. which had been unused for a long time, now found fresh favour in the summer sunshine.

I was particularly pleased about this, as it kept the children from the alternative attraction of scaling the coke pile, and also from the dark overgrown corner where a number of young birds were making their first forays.

As for Simon, it gave him an extra chance to shine, and I felt sure that this was an excellent thing to help him back to a normal life. The news from home, I gathered from the Mawnes, was dispiriting. Teresa remained in the nursing home, David struggled along on his own, his wife's treatment was hideously expensive and very little progress towards recovery seemed to have been made.

I felt extremely sorry for all of them. The Mawnes looked exhausted. They were not used to children in the house, and of course they were over anxious about young Simon. It could not have been easy for the child either. The Mawnes' house was full of exquisite furniture and expensive carpets, and a boy, even one as comparatively docile as young Simon, must have been a hazard among their treasures.

He had no other child to play with during the long light evenings. The Mawnes did not seem to think of inviting others as companions, or perhaps they felt that they could not face the responsibility. I wished that some of the parents would ask the child to play with their own, but the fact that Simon was staying at 'the big house' may have made them shy of offering an invitation.

The result was that the boy was definitely lonely. I noticed an odd streak in his character, as the time passed. He was easily made jealous.

If I praised someone's drawing, Simon would thrust his own before me. If I singled out one child to be a monitor, Simon would cast a look of bitter loathing in my direction. It was a difficult situation, and ignoring it was not enough, I felt.

Here was a damaged child who had watched his mad mother destroy his treasures before his eyes. He had been the object of her resentment and hatred. Was it any wonder that he too resented anything which drew praise and attention away from himself?

On the other hand, I could not afford to show favouritism, and justice must be done to my permanent pupils. I was particularly anxious that no resentment towards the newcomer should build up. They were a friendly and tolerant collection of children, but one could not expect them to put up with flashes of bad temper.

One instance had put me on my guard. Patrick had drawn a splendid map of Fairacre, a perfect riot of colour, and his industry had earned it pride of place on the wall. Inexplicably, it was found torn in half on the floor. No one would own up to its damage, and as Patrick seemed quite happy when we had mended it with adhesive tape, the matter was dropped, but I felt pretty sure that this was Simon's doing. I sensed too, that the children suspected him. Although this particular cloud blew over, I could not see many such incidents occurring without some retaliation. I could only hope for calm weather ahead.

We continued to see the robin family about, sometimes in the playground, but more often in my garden at the school house.

One unforgettable moment for me came one summer evening when I was washing up at the kitchen sink, and watching through the window the coming and going of blackbirds, thrushes, greenfinches, and a host of tits. The garden seemed full of activity, when suddenly the white robin appeared and perched on a branch of an old plum tree some yards from the window.

The ancient gnarled bark had exuded a sizeable drop of golden resin, over the last few months, and this was illuminated by the rays of the sunset, glowing like some precious bead of amber.

It exactly matched the colour of the robin's red breast, fiery against the purity of its white feathers. The two spots of warm ambience were a joy to see, one enhancing the other, until the bird flew off again with a whirring of snowy wings, and only the glowing gum remained to remind me of it.

By July the weather was really hot, and we were all beginning to long for some rain for our parched gardens. The children found the heat trying at midday, and I had to shift my desk from under the direct rays of sunshine through the skylight.

The shady corner abutting on to the vicar's wall became a popular spot to play, and the deck quoits were shifted into the shady part of the playground. Quite a number of the children elected to take a book under the trees which border the field next to the school during their dinner hour, for the unusual heat did not encourage them to race about in their normal fashion.

Simon, with his fair colouring, seemed to feel the heat more than most of his companions, and moved restlessly about in his desk, sighing at intervals.

One brilliant morning of exceptional heat, he was more fidgetty than usual. The schoolroom door was propped open to get any air available, and the children had a clear view of the mealworm tin.

Now that the young birds appeared to be capable of looking for their own food, there were fewer visitors to the tin, but the white robin still made occasional trips, and this morning I realised from the sudden cessation of my class's activities and the rapt attention on their faces that he had arrived several times.

When Simon asked to be excused I was glad to let him go. A walk across the playground might make him settle to his work more readily when he returned.

He was gone for some time. In his absence, the robin must have come once more to the tin, for the children's pens remained poised, and their eyes were fixed on the playground.

Suddenly, there was a sharp cry from Ernest and a horrified gasp from the class at large. To my astonishment, the children rose as one man and surged towards the door, with Ernest in the lead. I leapt forward to see what was going on.

There, at the side of the tin, lay the white robin, a deck quoit hard by. In the shade, near the lavatories, stood Simon, another quoit like a bracelet on his arm. He stood absolutely still, white and shaken, but there was a gleam in his blue eyes which, to my mind, showed triumph.

It was Ernest who picked up the robin. He passed it to me, but continued to stroke the beautiful feathers. It was plain that the bird's neck was broken. Its tiny body lay

warm and pathetic in the palm of my hand, and the children stood close to me, their faces anguished and their eyes fixed upon their dead friend.

It was Ernest who broke the silence with a most appalling howling noise. The tears burst from his eyes and sobs racked his body.

The sight of Ernest, the biggest, the calmest, the most reliable boy in the school, reduced to such a state seemed to galvanise the rest of them into action. They turned towards Simon and surrounded him before I had time to reach the child.

When I saw their faces, contorted with fury, I realised how a mob bent upon lynching must look.

For one moment, I feared that I had lost control of my children, but pushing between them, still holding the dead bird, I ordered them to go into school.

They hardly heard me at first, so intent were they upon wreaking vengeance, but gradually one or two began to make their way to the schoolroom door. There were tears on most cheeks now, and I looked at Simon.

He was dry eyed, but obviously terror stricken. As I watched him, he took a deep shuddering breath, and slipped to the ground in a dead faint.

At that moment, the infants' teacher appeared, alerted by the fracas.

'Settle them inside,' I begged her, 'and then come and help me with the boy.'

Five minutes later, Simon was lying on my couch in the school house. The white robin lay motionless on the window sill, its dead red breast aflame in the sunshine.

My assistant had returned to her double duty, and I went to the telephone.

'Henry,' I said when Mr Mawne answered, 'we are in terrible trouble here. Can you come at once?'

CHAPTER 8

Fairacre Mourns

I was extremely sorry to have to add to the Mawnes' worries, and waited for Henry's arrival with considerable agitation.

I had explained briefly on the telephone about the sad event. It was going to hit Henry doubly hard, I was afraid, both on Simon's account and the rare albino robin's.

The boy still lay listlessly on the couch, his small hands folded on his chest. They looked too fragile to have dealt that deadly blow which would soon shatter the joy of Fairacre.

The crunch of tyres on gravel announced Henry's arrival. I went to meet him, lifting the pathetic corpse from the window sill, and putting it into the patch pocket of my cotton frock.

Henry looked even more shaken than young Simon. I took him to the boy's couch. Henry touched the pale hair gently.

'Feeling better?'

The boy shook his head, and his mouth began to quiver.

It might be a good thing, I thought, if the tears of remorse came now. But the child remained dry eyed and silent.

'Come and have a look at the garden,' I said to Henry, 'while Simon's resting.'

I took him out of earshot. We sat on the garden seat, out of Simon's sight, and I withdrew the little corpse from my pocket.

Henry took it in his hands very tenderly. He seemed considerably closer to weeping than the boy we had left indoors.

'I wouldn't have had this happen for all the tea in

China,' he muttered. 'And to think Simon did it! It makes it so much more horrible. Tell me what happened.'

I explained, while Henry nodded thoughtfully.

'He's an uncanny shot,' he said, 'and that allied to his unpredictable temper makes him a dangerous child, I fear.'

He sighed heavily.

'Sometimes I think he's abnormal. Like his poor mother.'

'He's only abnormal in that he's badly hurt just now. He'll grow out of these tantrums. At the moment he craves attention. That accounts for these violent flashes of jealousy – envy of any child who gets more than he does, and envy of any other object, even an innocent robin, if it is admired.'

'You're kind,' said Henry, 'but I'm past comfort at the moment.'

He held out the robin to me.

'I'll put it in the garden shed, and bury it later on,' I said. 'I've no doubt the children will want to know what's happened to it, but I'm sure none of us can face a harrowing bird funeral, which one or two might favour.'

We walked together through the sunlit garden.

'But what's to be done?' asked Henry. 'The boy can't stay at school, obviously. When does term end?'

'In less than two weeks. And I must say, I think you're right about keeping Simon out of the way of the other children. They are an easy-going lot normally, but this has upset them dreadfully, and I wouldn't like to answer

92

for the consequences. Besides, the child needs rest – nursing, one might almost say. If you and Elizabeth can manage it, I should think he would soon recover with you. I take it David can't have him?'

'Impossible at the moment, and Teresa is no better. She gets these destructive moods, I gather, and they are having to treat her with some sort of tranquillisers. She's done a lot of damage to her room.'

He sighed again, and I felt helpless to comfort him. Truth to tell, I was in a state of shock myself, and was doing my best to control involuntary trembling.

'What an unhappy family!' cried Henry. 'Well, we must do what we can. Thank God, the child goes to prep school in September. He needs an entirely fresh start.'

'He can rest here for another hour or two, if you like,' I offered.

'No, no. You have been more than kind, but you have all the other children to see to. It's a sad day for them all. I'll take Simon back in the car, and we'll get him to bed, and call the doctor. I must get in touch with David tonight when he gets home. Poor boy! He has nothing but trouble.'

Simon was still prone on the couch when we entered, but sat up when Henry said they would be going home.

He was still pale, and seemed shaky as he accompanied his uncle to the door.

He said no word until he reached the car. Then he turned and proffered a small hand – the same hand that had killed our dear robin. I took it in mine.

'Thank you for looking after me,' he said politely, and then clambered in beside Henry.

I watched them drive away. Was that the last I should see of poor young Simon, I wondered?

Well, he was in safe hands, I told myself, and there were others to try and comfort now.

I returned to school with a heavy heart.

The news of the robin's death upset the inhabitants of Fairacre far more severely than I had imagined.

Country people are attuned to violent ends among animals, and can meet these tragedies with stoical calm. But somehow, the white robin had meant more to them than just another garden bird.

I think that the fact that it had created so much interest in the wider world, after Henry's article and the television programme, made the Fairacre folk intensely proud of their rare visitor. Of course they were genuinely fond of the albino – their doting looks and eager enquiries were proof of that – but without Henry's enthusiasm their interest would have been less keen.

How much he meant was brought home to me sharply by seeing, for the first time, tears in Mrs Pringle's normally stony eyes. I felt profoundly shocked. She had ministered to the bird right from the start, zealously bringing the mealworms he so enjoyed, but I had not realised how devoted she had been to him.

The children were inconsolable, and surprisingly mild in their remarks about Simon's part in the tragedy. Had he been present it might have been a different story, and I was glad that he was safely at the Mawnes'. I had not forgotten the ugly scene immediately after the bird's death.

I was relieved too that they did not demand a funeral for the bird, and accepted the fact that I had buried the corpse near the box hedge. But when Ernest arrived one morning with a somewhat rickety wooden cross bearing the words:

OUR SNOWBOY

and pleaded for it to be erected on the grave, I had not the heart to refuse. If it gave the children some comfort, then why not?

About a week after the sad event, Amy rang up. She too had heard about the albino bird. News travels fast in the country, I know, but I was surprised that it had travelled so far and so quickly.

'I don't know why you should be,' said Amy, when I remarked on it. 'My window cleaner has connections with Fairacre, and he keeps me up to date with the news. What a horrible shock for you all. What happened?'

I told her, my tongue loosened by her unexpected sympathy. Amy had treated our absorbed interest in the bird with some amusement. I think she felt we were somewhat ridiculous, but now that disaster had come she could not have been kinder.

'Heavens! That makes the whole affair much worse. May I tell Irene Umbleditch?'

'Who?' I said, bewildered.

'You know,' said Amy impatiently. 'You met her brother Horace here.'

'Sorry, sorry! The organist, of course. I remember he mentioned a sister who knew Simon.'

'Well, she's staying with her brother at the moment, and he is standing in for your organist next Sunday, and I said I'd drive him over this evening to try the organ. He's picking up the key from Mr Annett at Beech Green as we come through. It's such a lovely evening, I thought Irene might enjoy the drive too. Can we call to see you?'

'Please do. And certainly tell her if you want to. It's no secret, I'm afraid, but the child is being kept well away from everyone until his father can collect him.'

'Best thing to do,' said Amy heartily. 'He'd probably be torn limb from limb if he encountered any of your pupils in the village.'

I was about to protest indignantly at this slight on my children, but Amy cut me short.

'See you later then,' she said, and rang off.

I took to Irene Umbleditch as soon as we met. She was small and plump with soft dark hair. No one could call her pretty, but she had a sweetness of expression, and a low musical voice which made her instantly attractive.

We women were left together when Horace departed towards the church, and we wandered round the garden enjoying the warm evening air.

Irene stopped by Ernest's lop-sided cross, and looked enquiringly at me.

'Are they still upset?'

'I'm afraid so. Nothing quite so tearful as when it first happened, but they often mention the robin, and I know they have great hopes of another white one some day.'

'And Simon?'

'They hardly mention him.'

'I meant do you see anything of him? I know he's still with his Uncle Henry.'

'Oh, now and again. He doesn't look very happy, but one could never call the child robust.'

She nodded.

'I should very much like to see him. We always got on well when I did a little baby-minding for Teresa and David. Perhaps Horace would let me call while I'm staying with him.'

'Why not see if they are free this evening?' suggested Amy.

'Let's ring up,' I said. 'I expect Simon's still up on a lovely evening like this, and if not you can arrange another meeting.'

Irene looked a little hesitant, but finally agreed, and we went indoors.

'Shall I get the number?' I asked. Since the tragedy, I had become only too familiar with it.

'Please,' said Irene.

Henry answered. He sounded somewhat bewildered.

'Sorry, I can't hear properly. This line's poor. Just a

minute while I put on my spectacles. I always hear better when I'm wearing them.'

I waited patiently, listening to various clicks and mutters as the search went on. At last he spoke again.

'Right! Who did you say?'

'Miss Umbleditch wants to speak to you, She's here with me.'

'Miss Umbleditch? Oh, *Irene*! Good, put her on, please.'

I handed over the instrument with some relief, and rejoined Amy in the garden.

'She's a nice woman,' I remarked.

'Very. Must have been much appreciated when she was a nanny.'

'Why? Isn't she one now?'

'I know she's looking for a permanency in the near future, but I gather she gave up when old Mrs Umbleditch became senile, and stayed with her. She died last month, I'm told, so now Irene's free to find another job.'

We sat on the garden seat in companionable silence. The rooks were flying homeward, and far away some sheep bleated. It was all very peaceful. A heavenly smell of roses and pinks wafted around us, and somewhere, far above, a late lark carolled away before going to bed. How lovely to live in Fairacre, I thought, for the umpteenth time! I never wanted to leave it, and with any luck I could be transported the few yards from the school house to the nearby graveyard with the minimum of fuss.

I was indulging myself with pleasantly melancholy thoughts of a few sorrowing pupils following my coffin, and trying to decide if it should be a spring or autumn occasion (I was jolly well not going to peg out in high summer!), and had already settled for *Ye Holy Angels Bright* as a good rousing hymn, when Irene returned from the telephone.

'I've said I'll walk down immediately,' she said, her eyes were bright. 'I had a word with Simon too. It was lovely to hear him.'

'I'll run you down,' said Amy, overcoming polite protests. 'You don't know where they live.'

'Well, I'll walk back. Horace should be finished within the hour.'

It was settled that we would all meet again for a drink at my house, and I went to get a tray ready while Amy and Irene departed. On the way, I picked up the heavy china *Gentleman's Relish* jar which had held the mealworms for Snowboy and his friends. I had put it on the window ledge on the day of the tragedy, but it was in a precarious position there, and would be safer put away in the garden cupboard.

Would it ever be used again, I wondered, as I rinsed it under the tap? I did not intend to leave it in the playground. The school bird table, and my own, would provide adequate feeding space, and the white china pot was too poignant a reminder of our lost robin.

A wave of indignation assailed me as the tap ran. That damned boy! Why should we all have been robbed of our lovely bird? And why should the bird itself have been robbed of its joy in flight, in exploring the hedges and gardens of Fairacre, and its growing pleasure in its human friends? Really, it struck at the very roots of justice, I told myself crossly.

Ah well, I sighed, replacing the pot on its allotted shelf, it's an unfair world!

The sound of Amy's car returning brought me back to my immediate duties, and I fetched the tray.

There was a beautiful sunset as we sipped our drinks.

Horace was enthusiastic about the organ at Fairacre church, but doubtful about the organ blower in the vestry.

'If it was Ernest,' I told him, 'he will be absolutely reliable.'

'No, this one was called Patrick,' said Horace. 'Ernest was having his hair cut, but will be there on Sunday.'

'Then you have nothing to fear,' I assured him.

'And how did you find Simon?' enquired Horace of his sister.

She turned from admiring the sunset, still dazzled by the blaze across the sky.

'Very sweet, but not well at all. As a matter of fact, I may as well tell you now, I've offered to look after him until he starts school in September.'

Her brother looked startled.

'But what about the jobs you were applying for?'

'They can wait,' said his sister calmly.

'I'm sure the Mawnes would be much relieved,' I ventured.

'Oh, nothing's definite yet. David will have to make

the decision of course. I think Mr Mawne will be in touch with him this evening, but that child wants looking after.'

'You're right about that,' I said.

And no one, I thought privately, is better able to do it than Irene Umbleditch.

CHAPTER 9

A Second Shock

Term ended a day or two after the visit of the Umbleditch pair, and I went away almost immediately.

A favourite aunt of mine lives in Dorset, and I was with her for three weeks, relishing her astringent views on life in general, and trying to keep up with her outstanding physical energy. Although she is in her seventies she gardens, walks and cycles, chattering the while, and is game for a brisk hand of whist or bridge until midnight. My own life at Fairacre seemed a rest cure in contrast.

Things seemed remarkably quiet when I returned and, of course, I knew nothing of the result of Irene Umbleditch's offer to the Mawnes. I did not have to wait long.

One of my first jobs was to go to the post office and the village shop. The morning was young and dewy. Later it would be really hot, I noted with satisfaction, but the freshness of the morning air brought out goose pimples on my bare arms, as I made my way through the village.

Outside the post office Henry Mawne's car was standing,

and inside sat Elizabeth. She looked very smart in navy blue with a moiré silk turban to match.

'We're just off to catch the 9.45,' she said, glancing at her watch, 'but I wish Henry would hurry. As usual, we discovered at the last minute that we had about ten pence in the house, so he has just gone to ask Mr Lamb to cash a cheque.'

'You've chosen a nice day for a spree,' I said.

'No spree unfortunately. Far from it, in fact. David rang last night. His wife died suddenly.'

'No! How dreadful!'

'Luckily, Irene is looking after Simon, so that should help.'

At this point, Henry emerged, stuffing notes into his wallet and looking agitated.

'Don't dare stop,' he called, struggling with his seat belt. 'Got to catch the train.'

With a roar they were off to Caxley, and I went into the post office to buy stamps.

Mr Lamb was alone, and looking unusually grave.

'Heard the news, I suppose?'

'Mrs Mawne told me that Teresa Mawne had died.'

'Did she tell you how?'

'Well, no.'

'Threw herself off the roof of that nursing home evidently.'

'Threw herself?' I echoed aghast.

'Mr Mawne said she's been very violent of late. Seems she broke away from her nurse, rushed up to this roof garden place, nipped over the railings and dropped.'

We gazed at each other in shocked silence.

'Best thing really,' said Mr Lamb at last.

'But ghastly for the family.'

'It is now. But won't be in the long run. There was no future for that poor soul anyway. She was bound to come to some violent end. Had it written in her face.'

This was so close to my own private feelings that I could find nothing to say.

'And what can I do for you?' enquired Mr Lamb, resuming his usual brisk manner.

I told him, and watched him tearing out the stamps with his deft careful fingers. How comforting everyday jobs were in times of shock!

We wished each other goodbye, and I continued on my way to the grocer's in more sober mood.

I was careful to say nothing about the Mawnes' loss. As far as I knew, only they, Mr Lamb and I had heard about Teresa's death. If suicide were the cause, then the family might well wish the matter to be kept quiet. No doubt young Simon would be kept in the dark about this aspect of the tragedy. He would be hard enough hit, in any case, by the loss of his mother, little though she had contributed to the child's happiness.

But, versed in the ways of village communication, I was not surprised to hear from Mr Willet that Teresa's end was common knowledge in the community. Well, I thought, at least the news wasn't leaked by me.

Mr Willet had offered to take some geranium cuttings for me and 'to bring 'em on at home', for which I was sincerely grateful. He visited me, sharp knife in hand, one afternoon towards the end of the holidays.

'She was a poor tool, that one,' remarked Mr Willet, referring to David's late wife. 'He got caught in a tangle of fair hair when he was young. Not the first neither. Blondes has a way with 'em. Still, it's sad to see her end this way.'

I agreed, watching Mr Willet's horny hand holding the geraniums aside with great delicacy as he searched for suitable cuttings.

'Can't wonder that boy turned out such a varmint,' he went on conversationally. 'If I'd have been there when our robin was killed I'd have given that boy the biggest larruping of his borns.'

'He fainted as it was,' I protested.

'Ah! And he'd have fainted a dam' sight quicker with me around! What about the other kids? They were upset enough, in all conscience! I bet they'd have set about him proper if you hadn't been there. We hear 'em, my missus and me, still talking about their Snowboy. It was a cruel wicked thing to do, and they don't forget it. Come to that, neither do us old 'uns.'

'We all miss him,' I said, 'but there was no point in letting the school run riot once the deed was done.'

'All I can say is, I hope that blasted boy don't show his face in Fairacre no more. We've seen enough of that one. I'm sorry about his ma, of course, but that don't alter what he done. I can't bring meself to forgive him, that I can't.'

'I thought you were a Christian,' I said.

'Well, I may be. But I'm what they call a militant one,' replied Mr Willet, snipping energetically.

'Do militant Christians drink tea?' I asked.

Mr Willet smiled.

'Try 'em,' he said.

A few evenings later, Amy called to tell me about an organ recital being given by Horace Umbleditch to raise funds for Bent church.

'It's the roof fund again,' said Amy, accepting a glass of sherry. 'We hover between the roof and the organ at Bent. If it's not one cracking up, it's the other.'

She surveyed her sherry with approval.

'You didn't win this at a fête,' she commented. 'What happened to the cough linctus?'

'You hogged most of that,' I told her. 'I was driven to spending my hard-earned cash on a bottle of Harvey's.'

'Well, you couldn't have done better,' said Amy kindly. 'Have I told you the latest about Horace?'

I hoped she was not going to tell me more about Teresa Mawne. It was time the poor soul was left in peace, I felt.

'What about him?' I said cautiously. Amy had that speculative look in her eye, which I know from experience goes with her match-making efforts.

'He's moving into a house at the school.'

'What school?'

Amy tut-tutted testily.

'The school he works at! Surely, you knew he was the music master at Maytrees?'

'The first I've heard of it.'

'Rubbish! I'm sure I told you *all* about him when he first came to Bent.'

'Honestly, I had no idea he taught. I just thought he was the organist at your church.'

'And very fat he'd get on *that* salary,' said Amy. 'Of course he had to have a job somewhere, and I'm sure I told you all about it. You don't listen half the time.'

'Well, I will now,' I said magnanimously. 'Fire away! So he teaches at Maytrees Prep School, and is going to live there.'

'That's right. There wasn't a house available in the grounds when he was appointed, which is why he had to go into those wretched digs. But now the classics man has retired and there's a nice little house free.'

'Good. More sherry?'

'You'd like it there,' said Amy.

'I'm not likely to be asked to visit very often, I imagine.'

Amy sighed.

'I wish you weren't so *prickly*. Here's a very nice young man – well, perhaps not *young*, but quite spry – and I really think he would like to be married –'

'Amy,' I broke in, 'you are nothing but a meddlesome busybody! How do you know he wants to get married?

Like me, he's probably perfectly happy as he is. And in any case, there are lots of more suitable candidates for the honour if he is intending matrimony.'

'Hoity-toity!' cried Amy. 'Very well, I promise never to mention marriage again!'

'Thank God!' I replied.

'But you will come and have a drink before the recital?' said Amy, picking up her bag. 'Horace will be there, of course, and our new doctor who is quite devastatingly good looking, and needs *friends*.'

'Thank you, Amy,' I said resignedly.

During the summer, the bird tables had been less used, but at the beginning of September an unusually chilly spell of weather brought some of our friends back, including several young robins.

The children showed their usual interest, but not surprisingly the name of Snowboy cropped up frequently.

They mourned the beautiful bird with genuine sorrow. He had been a rare and exciting visitor. The mere fact that he had been with us for a comparatively short spell made the memory of him doubly dear. The violence of his end made that memory doubly poignant.

As well as remarks about the dead robin, both verbal and written, there were innumerable pictures made, and even one or two poems. I had tried not to encourage too much harping on our lost albino, hoping that the children's natural exuberance would lessen their grief as the weeks went by, but on the other hand, it seemed to give them some comfort to remember him in various ways, and I thought it best to let the subject wear itself out naturally.

The weather helped. September developed into a warm golden period. With the harvest in, the farmers were busy ploughing, with a retinue of gulls and rooks following the lengthening chocolate-brown furrows.

The children played outside day after day, and our nature walks became more frequent. Before long, the winds of autumn and blizzards of winter would keep us confined within the ancient walls of the little school. We might as well get all the fresh air and exercise while we could, I felt.

This halcyon spell pleased Mrs Pringle too. The floors kept cleaner than usual, and the lighting of the tortoise stoves could be postponed, saving work in bringing in coke from the playground to feed the monsters. She became positively mellow, and I wondered privately if she were sickening for something.

She even offered to come and clean the windows of the school house one evening, and told me the Fairacre news as I rewarded her efforts with a cup of strong tea.

After a brief survey of the vicar's recent bout of indigestion ('Too much lardy cake for his age'), her niece Minnie's indisposition ('Another baby on the way') and the aggravating habits of her immediate neighbour ('Dragged up in the slums of London, so what could you expect?'), she turned to the young slayer of our lamented robin.

'Never could take to that boy,' said Mrs Pringle. 'Sly! Couldn't trust him, I always said. Looked as though butter wouldn't melt in his mouth, and then he done a wicked thing like that.'

'He'd had a pretty raw deal one way and another,' I pointed out.

'So what? I gets tired of people making excuses for other folks' wicked ways. When I was a girl there was Right and Wrong, and you got a good hiding if you Done Wrong, and not much praise if you Done Right! You should've Done Right anyway, was how my ma and pa looked at it!'

'But things aren't quite as simple as that,' I began, but Mrs Pringle ignored me. You might just as well try to dam the River Thames with a matchstick as to stop Mrs Pringle's flow when she is in full spate.

'But nowadays no one Does Wrong, as far as I can make out. Look at that Mrs Coggs as was had up for stealing. What happened to her? "More to be pitied than blamed," everyone said. "Her with her blackguard of a husband and all them kids, and not very bright up top to begin with." Excuses, excuses! It ends up with no one reckoning to pay the price for Doing Wrong. We've got free will, ain't we? What's to stop us choosing Right? I gets proper fed up with all this namby-pamby way of going on.'

I must admit that a great deal of Mrs Pringle's forthright arguments appealed to me, but I did not intend to say so.

'In Simon's case, his poor mother's illness definitely had an effect on him.'

'Maybe. But he'd got a good dad, and a grown-up sister and two brothers. They could've helped, I should've thought.'

'I don't think they were at home then,' I said.

'No, they weren't. I taxed Mr Mawne with it one morning when I met him in the street.'

Trust our Mrs Pringle, I thought.

'Them Mawnes are too old to cope with a young boy. I told him so, and he said there wasn't no one else really free. The sister's married and lives in New Zealand, and one boy's in the army and pushed from pillar to post, as you might say, while I forget now where the younger one is. Cambridge, perhaps, or Oxford, or one of those college places where they idle away their time till they're too old to learn anything.'

I let this trenchant criticism of our revered universities pass without comment. I was still admiring Mrs Pringle's successful attempts to elicit information from her victims.

'Anyway,' continued my informant, struggling to her feet, 'it's a good thing that Miss Umblethingummy's taken on the child. Them Mawnes were at the end of their tether, and she looks capable of giving that young man a walloping when it's called for. Though no doubt she lets him get away with murder, like the rest of these folk who should know better!'

She gave me a dark look, summing up, without speech

this time, her opinion of those in authority, particularly headmistresses, who let sinners go unpunished.

The organ recital took place at the end of September, and I drove to Amy's along lanes already beginning to take on the beauty of early autumn.

Sprays of glossy blackberries arched from the hedges, and the hazel nuts were plumping up. The lime trees were beginning to shed a few lemon-coloured leaves, and the apples were turning from green to rosy ripeness. It was a time of year when nature showed its kindly side, and the knowledge of winter to come could be comfortably shelved.

Amy's garden blazed with dahlias, and the house was beautifully decorated with bowls full of the velvety blossoms. About two dozen people stood about admiring them, drinks in hand, when I arrived, and among them was Irene Umbleditch.

I made my way towards her. Her brother, elegant as ever, was surrounded by a number of friends. It was quite apparent that Horace had soon found his feet, despite Amy's early solicitude on his behalf.

Of course I enquired about Simon.

'He's settled in fairly well at school,' said Irene. 'We took him down about ten days ago, and the matron has been very kind and kept us in the know. She was told about Teresa. It seemed only right, and I must say, she's a wonderfully motherly person, and Simon seems to have taken to her.'

'He's bright enough,' I said. 'Now that he's settled, he should do very well academically.'

I did not intend to mention the robin incident. It was over and done with, as far as I was concerned, but Irene herself brought up the subject.

'It was an appalling thing to happen,' she said, her face very grave. 'The other children must have suffered dreadfully. Do they still talk about it?'

'About the robin, yes. But they don't speak of Simon.'

'I wonder if they still hold it against him?'

I was torn between the truth and sparing this nice woman's feelings.

'Well,' I began, 'I know they bitterly resent what happened, and they hear their parents and other grown ups discussing the affair, of course. But they are pretty good tempered, and I don't think they bear much of a grudge against Simon now, although they did at the time.'

She nodded.

'He won't speak about it. Whether he'd be willing to come and visit Fairacre again, I don't know, but it certainly wouldn't be wise to try it yet.'

I agreed, and asked her what her plans were now that the boy was at school. Her face lit up.

'I'm taking new babies by the month,' she said. 'You know, from birth on for a few weeks. It's just temporary nursing, my favourite age, and I can fit in Simon's Christmas holidays then, and perhaps his Easter one, if he still needs me.'

'I'm sure his father is very grateful,' I hazarded.

'He can do with all the help he can get,' said Irene soberly. 'I don't think many men could have coped with such misery as bravely as he has.'

'Now, you must come and meet Doctor Manning,' said Amy, bustling up. 'In another half an hour we must make our way to the church. I really believe every seat will be taken. It augurs well for the roof fund, doesn't it?'

CHAPTER 10

The Long Wait Over

Term rolled on. The usual autumn activities enlivened our school progress – harvest festival, the doctor's medical inspection and preparations for Christmas.

The glowing spell of weather broke at last to give several weeks of rough wind and driving rain. The bird tables were well patronised by chaffinches, greenfinches, blue tits, coal tits, marsh tits, and the ubiquitous sparrows and starlings.

The young robins now sported breasts almost as red as their older relatives, and were bold in coming to the table and looking out for any crumbs scattered by the children at playtime.

Since the advent and death of the albino bird the children took more notice of the robins, I thought. The hope of another white one in the spring was kindled anew as the time passed, and explained, in part, the extra cherishing that came the robins' way.

I mentioned this to Henry Mawne one cold January day when we met at a managers' meeting at the school.

'Well, don't raise their hopes too much,' he advised me. 'The chances are slight, you know. And I wonder if albino robins aren't better forgotten perhaps. A second tragedy would hurt them badly, and as you know, these albinos can get set upon pretty viciously by the normal birds.'

'Snowboy didn't,' I pointed out.

Henry sighed.

'No, I'm afraid he was set upon by the most vicious predator of all. Man has a lot to answer for.'

He looked so sad that I hastened to drop the subject, but bore his warning in mind.

He came back to the school house with me after the meeting, to collect some bird books I had borrowed.

'Simon all right?' I asked.

'Looking fine. We saw them over Christmas, you know. Seems to like his school, and had a cautiously optimistic report. The head's a kindly sort of chap, and knows about the boy's background. In fact, I told him about the robin. Perhaps I shouldn't have done, but he was such a sympathetic listener, I'm afraid I let it out.'

And probably did you a world of good to do so, I thought. Aloud I said:

'What did he say?'

'Nothing. But he's going to put the boy in charge of the frogspawn, and I bet those tadpoles will be guarded against all comers.'

'He'll enjoy this term then. He's back, I suppose?'

'Yes, David and Irene took him down last week. That

girl is an angel. She came in every day to look after things during the holiday, and it's made all the difference to the child. And to David,' he added, as though he had just realised it.

'I liked her enormously,' I said, 'and hope I shall see her again some time.'

'Won't be for a bit,' said Henry. 'She's off to a case at the end of the month, and thoroughly looking forward to it. Seems strange to me. New babies are so *unfinished*, aren't they?'

'No worse than newly hatched birds,' I said. 'They're positively *grisly* without feathers.'

A look which can only be described as maudlin spread over Henry's features.

'They're *perfect*,' he told me, and I did not contradict him.

Excitement began to mount towards the end of term as the nesting season began. I did my best to warn the children against over optimism, with Henry's words in mind, but I was up against fierce hope, and who could be too daunting after all that they had suffered?

We watched the robins in particular, of course. On two occasions we saw a female fluttering her wings and begging for food, while the male bird fed her attentively. We could not be sure if it was the same pair, but rather hoped that there were two couples. It doubled our chances.

The children were not alone in their hopes. Mrs Pringle

had no doubt at all that we should have another albino this time.

'Very possibly two or more,' she pronounced, in the hearing of the children, which alarmed me slightly.

'You'd best get out that mealworm dish again,' she told me. 'Might as well do it now. Get 'em used to bringing their babies along.'

Mr Willet was equally positive.

'If it's happened once it'll happen again. Didn't Mr Mawne say so?'

I responded that Henry had warned us not to hope, but my fears were dismissed disdainfully.

Mr Lamb, Mr Partridge, the Misses Waters, the Hales, Miss Quinn, and in fact everyone in Fairacre, it seemed, awaited the arrival of another albino robin with supreme confidence. I trembled for them.

As far as I could make out, the robins were not nesting in my garden this spring. Henry Mawne had *carte blanche* to roam about it whenever he so wished, in his researches, but he agreed that there seemed to be no sign of a robin's nest, though he had discovered two blackbirds', a tit's and two thrushes' abodes.

The vicar's garden, he told me, seemed more promising, and the bosky corner near the lavatories was under his particular surveillance. I told the children about this, and they obligingly hurried from the lavatories and tried to resist the temptation of lingering in their favourite hiding place. Any embryo albino robin in our vicinity was getting every consideration.

In the end, Henry discovered two robins' nests. One was just over the dividing wall among the vicar's neglected weeds. The other at the far end of the vicar's garden towards the churchyard. We waited avidly for further developments.

Obediently I had put the *Gentleman's Relish* jar back in the playground, in full view of the class. Mrs Pringle kept it supplied with mealworms, and we had a generous number of bird visitors, including robins. Some days I refused to have the door propped open because of the draught, and the children eyed me resentfully on these occasions.

Their anxiety was summed up, I felt, by one brief incident. They were busy painting one afternoon and the room was blissfully quiet.

Patrick looked up from his work.

'What if we don't?' he enquired.

'Don't what?' I replied, connecting his remark with his artistic efforts.

'Get a white 'un,' he enlarged, ignoring his paint brush dripping wet paint.

As one man, the class rounded on this Doubting Thomas within their midst.

' 'Course we'll get one!'

'Maybe two. Mrs Pringle said so!'

'Shut up, you old misery!'

'Us had one before, didn't us? Well then!'

Patrick quailed before the onslaught, and I had to calm the rabble.

Peace was soon restored, but it was a startling display of undaunted hope. Would it be justified?

It was at the beginning of the summer term that the excitement became intense. Three young robins were seen by the mealworm dish being fed by their parents. Handsome though they were, they were welcomed with modified rapture by the children.

Could there be an albino among this brood which had not yet been seen? Had the second clutch hatched yet? Was there a white robin among it? How soon should we know the worst? Or best?

It was Mrs Partridge, the vicar's wife, who raised our hopes to even more exalted heights. The vicar passed on the news to me in the lobby, shutting the classroom door with some care.

'I should be sorry to raise their hopes falsely,' he assured me, 'but my wife certainly had a glimpse of something white among those deplorable nettles by my compost heap. Of course, we're keeping a sharp watch from the hide. If only Henry were here!'

We all echoed the vicar's heart cry. Everyone in Fairacre had been bitterly disappointed when Henry had been asked, at short notice, to take over another birdwatching expedition, this time to Turkey. Mrs Pringle, in particular, looked upon his departure as downright treachery.

'Should have thought his place was here with our robins,' she said, 'not gadding off to some foreign place where the birds can't understand the Queen's English.'

Her feelings were shared by all in Fairacre, but not so roundly expressed.

I returned to my children, surprised to find that I was trembling with excitement at the vicar's disclosure. Could it be? Could Mrs Partridge really have seen an albino robin? Or was it, as I had first thought on hearing of Helen Coggs's sighting of Snowboy, just a flutter of white paper or a nodding blossom?

The day was fine, and I propped open the door. The mealworms writhed in their unlovely way in the depths of the china pot. A robin came, dived in his beak, and flew off to feed his family.

The children were copying a notice from the blackboard. It was to be taken home, announcing the times of our school Open Days, and they were doing their best to write legibly, so that their parents would have no cause for complaint.

It was Ernest who saw it first, and how right and proper it was that he should be the one whose eye first lighted upon our little miracle.

Quite alone, the white robin stood, legs askew, and dark eyes cocked upon the mealworms. His snowy feathers gleamed in the sunshine, his speckled breast glowing against the shining white satin of his young plumage.

'He's come,' whispered Ernest, standing up. Behind him the rest of the children rose too, the better to see their long-awaited visitor. Their faces were rapt, their eyes as bright as the white robin's.

Without hurry, fearless in his beauty, the white robin selected a mealworm, spread his dazzling wings into two perfect fans, and made off towards the vicar's wall.

Joyous pandemonium broke out in the class room. Children thumped their neighbours. Children hugged each other. Children crowded round my desk, and made enough noise to raise the roof. We might have been at a football match for all the emotional fervour shown.

In the midst of it, Mrs Pringle entered, black oil cloth bag on arm.

'He's come!' they yelled, surging towards her. 'Another white robin! He's come again!'

Solid as the Rock of Gibraltar amidst the waves of children tumbling around her, Mrs Pringle stood unmoved.

Above the hubbub her voice boomed triumphantly.

'Well, what did I tell you?'